THE

SPACE

BETWEEN

OUR

FOOTSTEPS

Landscape, Riham Ghassib

THE SPACE BETWEEN OUR FOOTSTEPS

Poems and Paintings

from the Middle East

SELECTED BY

NAOMI SHIHAB NYE

SIMON & SCHUSTER BOOKS FOR YOUNG READERS

A NOTE TO READERS:

OVER 500 "CALLS FOR ENTRIES" WERE MAILED, FAXED, AND E-MAILED TO POETS, ARTISTS, CULTURAL INSTITUTIONS, UNIVERSITIES, AND GALLERIES IN THE MIDDLE EAST. WE ARE GRATEFUL TO THE MANY INDIVIDUALS AND INSTITUTIONS WHO RESPONDED.

THE EDITORS WOULD ALSO LIKE TO EXPRESS SINCERE AND LASTING THANKS TO SALWA MIKDADI NASHASHIBI OF THE CULTURAL AND VISUAL ARTS RESOURCE. MS. NASHASHIBI WAS, FROM HER DESK IN JORDAN, AN INVALUABLE AND EXPERT SLEUTH. THIS BOOK WOULD NOT HAVE BEEN POSSIBLE WITHOUT HER.

ABOUT THE ENDPAPERS:

EXCERPTS FROM SOME OF THE POEMS IN THIS ANTHOLOGY APPEAR ON THE ENDPAPERS IN THEIR ORIGINAL LANGUAGES: "VOICED LAMENT" BY GÜLTEN AKIN IN TURKISH, "SEA" BY SHAFEE'E KADKANI IN FARSI, "ZIAD'S LITTLE MOONS" BY MAMDOUH ADWAN IN ARABIC, AND "RICE PARADISE" BY RONNY SOMECK IN HEBREW.

SIMON & SCHUSTER BOOKS FOR YOUNG READERS
An imprint of Simon & Schuster Children's Publishing Division
1230 Avenue of the Americas, New York, New York 10020

Copyright © 1998 by Naomi Shihab Nye
Pages 131-137 constitute an extension of the copyright page.

SIMON & SCHUSTER BOOKS FOR YOUNG READERS is a trademark of Simon & Schuster.

Book design by Anahid Hamparian
The text of this book is set in 12-point Gilgamesh.
Map by Mike Regan

Printed and bound in Singapore
First Edition
10 9 8 7 6 5 4 3 2 1
Library of Congress Cataloging-in-Publication Data
The space between our footsteps : poems & paintings from the Middle East / selected by Naomi Shihab Nye.
p. cm.
Selected poetry from Arabic, Hebrew, Persian, and Turkish.
Summary: A collection of poetry and full-color artwork from Middle Eastern countries.
ISBN 0-689-81233-7
1. Young adult poetry—Translations into English. [1. Poetry—Collections.] I. Nye, Naomi Shihab.
PN6109.97.S63 1998
808.81'00835—dc21
97-18622
CIP
AC

In the spirit of the children at the Cairo library who said, during the worst sandstorm of the twentieth century,
"Just keep reading!"

from Letters to Childhood

Forgive me, my child,
if the name I gave you
is not the name
you would have chosen . . .

All the children of the world,
in all my abodes
you are the roses in my courtyard,
the green and the fresh,
the sun and the stars,
you are the beautiful hands,
the ones who raise the flag of childhood high.

I give my life to you.
To you I write my poems.

MOHAMMED SHEHADEH
Translated by Aziz Shihab

İNTRODUCTİON

Stop Neglecting Our Children, Salwa Arnous Elaydi

IF YOU SAY YOU ARE GOING to the Middle East, people around you often raise their eyebrows. It is quite possible that the Middle East is one of the most negatively stereotyped places on earth. How did this happen to a place which has been the center of so much dramatic cultural and religious history? Unless American adults and teenagers have lived or traveled in the region themselves, many know only what they hear in the news or see in flamboyant movies (Arabs riding out of the desert on horseback). Of course, the violent or unhappy news stories are usually the ones that get transmitted. But what a terrible fragment they are of the fuller story, which is as rich and interesting as life anywhere else.

We should remember that the same distortion of news is happening in the other direction, too. What do Middle Easterners hear and imagine about the United States? We are a country of murderers and drug addicts. People are afraid to walk in the streets. Families are fractured. Students are "dropping out" in all directions. We don't care about our elders, putting them in "homes" away from us. Most of us would resent such a negative portrait and would work hard to balance it.

I can't stop believing human beings *everywhere* hunger for deeper-than-headline news about one another. Poetry and art are some of the best ways this heartfelt "news" may be exchanged.

AS AN ARAB-AMERICAN CHILD growing up in the United States, I never read anything remotely connected to my father's first culture, except perhaps *The Arabian Nights.* This book hardly felt much like our *lives.*

Luckily, I had a fair imagination and our Palestinian father was a wonderful storyteller. Every night my brother and I drifted off to sleep wrapped in the mystery of distant neighbors, villages, ancient stone streets, donkeys, and olive trees. Our house by day was fragrant with cardamom spice and coffee, pine nuts sizzled in olive oil and delicious cabbage rolls. My girlfriends brought iced cupcakes to Girl Scouts for treats, but I brought dates, apricots, and almonds. Arabic music on scratchy records filled the air in our home.

I wasn't yet sure where the sense of "other" began in the human heart or how many variations and shadings the larger family could contain. But I didn't fear differences. In fact, I loved them. This is one of the best things about growing up in a mixed family or community. You never think only one way of doing or seeing anything is right.

After beginning high school in Jerusalem, which altered my perception of the universe irrevocably, then returning to the States to live in Texas, I began reading books by Khalil Gibran, one of the best-selling authors of all time. Teenagers often identify with his ruminative tone, lyrical philosophies, and eloquent sense of contradiction. I used to smuggle *The Prophet* into my homemaking class wrapped in the denim dress I was sewing. I would read it between stitches.

"Only when you drink from the river of silence shall you indeed sing" and "Your children are not your children./They come through you but not from you,/And though they are with you, yet they belong not to you . . . /You are the bows from which your children as living arrows are sent forth . . ."

Gibran came to the United States from Lebanon when he was 27 and devoted himself to writing in both Arabic and English, and to painting and drawing. Though he died at a relatively young age (48), his work outlives him in a powerful way, continuing to appear in new editions. The only park dedicated to a writer in Washington, D.C., was dedicated, within the past decade, to Gibran. It sits across the road from the Vice President's house. I think Gibran would be very happy to know that other Arab-American writers have been finding one another the past 20 years and a slowly, but steadily increasing, body of work by Middle Eastern writers is being made available to readers in the United States. We toast Gibran for his devotion and example.

Mother & Child, Baya Mahieddine

The History of Literature and art in the Middle East extends back countless generations. In tribal times poetry was recited around a blazing fire—a popular early tradition was the spoken add-on poem in which each voice contributed new lines, in turn. Repetition, passionate rhythm, and melodrama were admired.

This book in your hands (the word "anthology" comes from the Greek for "gathering of flowers") offers a medley of voices and visions from the twentieth century. Consider *The Space Between Our Footsteps* to be like the *mezza* tables of hors d'oeuvres spread out all across the Middle East, which often precede a greater feast—tiny, delicious plates of *hummos* and *baba ghanouj*, elegantly decorated with sprigs of mint and dashes of paprika, *tabbooleh* salad, pickled turnips, cucumbers and tomatoes, heaps of bread . . . guests dip in from all directions.

With writers and artists from Algeria, Bahrain, Egypt, Iran, Iraq, Israel, Jordan, Kuwait, Lebanon, Libya, Morocco, Oman, Palestine, Qatar, Saudi Arabia, Syria, Tunisia, Turkey, United Arab Emirates, and Yemen, our book has tried to represent the wide, delicious feast. In no way does it pretend to be comprehensive—it's neither "the whole garden" nor "the whole meal."

While some who like to classify might describe Middle Eastern poetry as being heavily embellished or romanticized and Middle Eastern art as being primarily abstract, this book hopes to extend that notion. Subjects include an immense affection for childhood and children, a tender closeness to family, a longing for early, more innocent days, a passion for one's homeland, grief over conditions of exile (a situation too common through the centuries to many Middle Easterners), a reverent regard for the natural world, and a love for one another and for daily life. Do any of these concerns sound alien to us?

◆ ◆ ◆

Once My Husband Michael and I were sleeping soundly in our room in an old downtown hotel in Aleppo, Syria, when the water in our bathroom sink turned on by itself. I woke gradually to the gush of a waterfall, the encroaching roar of a fountain, and couldn't imagine where the sound was coming from.

Slowly my eyes adjusted to the stream of water pouring from the edge of the sink onto our bathroom floor. It rolled riverlike into the bedroom so the rugs beside our bed were already soaked. I leapt into the bathroom and attempted to turn off the water. The faucet spun uselessly in my hand. How had this happened? Did our room have ghosts?

I grabbed the telephone. But my *SOS* Arabic at one A.M. wasn't very good. Soon the groggy desk clerk appeared at our door with a pitcher full of drinking water, thinking I'd *asked* for some. When he saw the sea growing rapidly around us, he awakened quickly, racing back to the old-fashioned metal-cage elevator with its ornate grillwork. He returned soon with a mop, a bucket, and a basket of rags and the three of us set to work, joined in our cause, until Michael pointed out it might be a good idea to turn off the water valve under the sink. We'd all been too sleepy to think of it.

The valve was stuck. The clerk ran for pliers. What happened next was like a dance, three people mopping, dipping, laughing, wringing out the rags, soaking our pajama cuffs and socks. The clerk shrugged when I kept asking him in my bumbling Arabic how this could have happened. Weren't we in the Middle East? Wasn't water something of a premium in these ancient lands? Maybe this was one of the springs that used to rise up suddenly between stones in my father's folktales.

We fell asleep again. At 4:30 A.M. our telephone rang and the clerk, now our good buddy, said someone was downstairs waiting for us. A plumber? We hadn't been expecting anyone. We dressed hurriedly and rode the clanky elevator down. A tall red-haired man shook our hands and introduced himself as Adlai Qudsi, architect and preservationist, who had come to give us a sunrise tour of his beloved city. We did not tell him we had already been up half the night, nor did we have the slightest inclination not to follow him.

He took us first to the famous citadel which towers over Aleppo like a castle with its fortress-wall. We could look down over the twinkling city from there. He took us walking in careful single file along the edges of rooftops to a sitting spot where we could watch the sky ease gently into its early, perfect pink. Who was this person who would dream up such an outing for people he didn't even know? He shrugged. "I heard some visitors were in town. I thought you might like to see something special." He showed us exactly where to gaze to get the best views of sky and buildings and land.

After sunrise, he knocked on doors in the Old City. Sleepy women wearing flowery aprons let us in. They obviously knew and respected Mr. Qudsi. He wanted to show us how the soft early light fell through their high arched windows, illuminating blue and green mosaic tiles. He wanted us to see a three-hundred-year-old fountain in a courtyard. Light fell onto its tower like a glittering top-hat. When we sat with Mr. Qudsi in a café for breakfast tea, we told about our water escapade and he grinned. "I'd much rather have old pipes than new buildings!" he said proudly.

THIS IS WHAT I WANT a book of poems and paintings to be—a surprising spring waking us from our daily sleep. A feast of little dishes. An unexpected walk along the rim of a majestic city. *Ahlan Wa Sahlan*—You are all welcome!

Naomi Shihab Nye
SAN ANTONIO, TEXAS

The Girl's Pride, Ahmad Nawash

"A galaxy of seeds"

Picture

Three girls in the family album.
Good-looking as they knew how to be
in Tyre, Lebanon, nineteen-thirty-eight.
Behind them are steps and an unsteady railing.
A flowerpot has been placed at their feet,
at the request of the refined photographer,
for the sake of the composition.

In the righthand corner a circle gleams
in the heart of the tile that, for years,
carried the burden of the flowerpot
with great courtesy.
Now, bare, it is exposed to its shame
before the camera.

It seems that after the click
no one will bother
to return the pot to its place.
And perhaps that tile carries
the ring of shame on its heart
to this very day.

I would not have committed the modest
memory of that flowerpot to paper
had it not, for a long time,
recurred in my dreams.

The girl in the middle is dressed in black.
In due time she will be my mother.

ANTON SHAMMAS
Translated by Judy Levy

Untitled, Wafaa al-Sabagh

Coda

They say in my village
I was born
With one hand placed
Over my heart
The men said
This child will live
With the heart of a prophet
And the women of the tribe

"Rejoice!" they said
Hailing the future lover
But the old men
Were holding back their tears
                    and keeping calm

SHAFIQ AL-KAMALI
Translated by Sargon Boulus and Christopher Middleton

Beginning Speech

That child I was
came to me once
an unfamiliar face

He said nothing—we walked
each glancing in silence at the other
One step
an alien river
                flowing.

Our common origins
            brought us together
and we separated
a forest written by the earth
and told by the seasons

Child that I once was, advance,
What now brings us together?
And what have we to say to each other?

ADONIS
Translated by Lena Jayyusi and John Heath-Stubbs

When I Was a Child

When I was a child
grasses and masts stood at the seashore,
and as I lay there
I thought they were all the same
because all of them rose into the sky above me.

Only my mother's words went with me
like a sandwich wrapped in rustling waxpaper,
and I didn't know when my father would come back
because there was another forest beyond the clearing.

Everything stretched out a hand,
a bull gored the sun with its horns,
and in the nights the light of the streets caressed
my cheeks along with the walls,
and the moon, like a large pitcher, leaned over
and watered my thirsty sleep.

YEHUDA AMICHAI
Translated by Stephen Mitchell

From This Star to the Other

My father is a laborer.
He comes to the farm
with the last star of the morning sky.
And returns home
with the first star of the evening sky.
My father is the sun!

SALMAN HARRATI
Translated by Fereshteh Gol-Mohammadi

from *Unveiled*

I have always known my place. "When I grow up, I want to become the wife of the president," I said. I also wanted to write books, drive a jeep, and have a dog as a best friend.

That I kept to myself.

♦ ♦ ♦

"Cover her face," my grandmother told my parents on our way to the beach. "She is already too dark."

"Where did you get such black hair?" she said, with obvious concern.

"From you, grandmother."

♦ ♦ ♦

"It must have confused you to get such attention just because of your sex," I told my brother, my mother's son.

"You must have cried laughing at such stupidity that you were better simply because you were a boy."

"I believed it," my brother said.

I have always wanted to topple my brother from his throne. I read, I intellectualized, I socialized, I schemed, I yelled, I cried, and in the end, I couldn't even compare.

♦ ♦ ♦

My brother was baptized in Jerusalem. A special boy, a special place. I was also baptized,

with my sister, by "Father Potatoes," so-called because he was really fat. Or at least, that is all my mother remembers from that joyous, local, and double event.

♦ ♦ ♦

There was money to be made at our dining room table. My mother put sterilized coins in her delicious *kibbe** dish. The trick was to pick the *kibbe* with the hidden coin. I never won. My brother won every time.

Later I realized the game was fixed. When confronted by a grown-up me, my mother didn't see what the fuss was about. "Your brother was a sickly boy who needed nourishment."

♦ ♦ ♦

My brother was an overweight bully.

♦ ♦ ♦

"But we love you," my parents said. "We love you very much." I know, but they loved me as a girl.

♦ ♦ ♦

The boy within me was stuck with me. Not till much later did I find out that the boy within was really a girl.

GLADYS ALAM SAROYAN

kibbe—popular casserole made of cracked wheat and meat

On the Other Side of a Glance, Reza De Rakshani

My Mother's Wedding Parade

Still a child, innocent, naïve, seventeen.
A good student pulled out of school to wed.
It was arranged, it was final, it was done.
The gown was rented, the whole town paraded.
The brief private talk with the aunt and
the stepmother took place—
very little was learned. Salimeh* was not relaxed.
She shook, she perspired, she cried,
she was a child.
The whole town brought sweets in their Sunday best.
She wept upon leaving her father's modern home
for a humble two-room stone house
to share with her in-laws and a man
she knew only by sight.

She went along, went along,
singing to herself a song of prayers.
The whole town looked on, gossiped,
and the wedding picture showed a different dress
from the original one—
a wrinkled dress.
My mother was so tall, so beautiful, so strong,
her dress was so long.

LORENE ZAROU-ZOUZOUNIS

*Salimeh—a girl's name

A Prayer

I was less than seven years old when I said a prayer for the revolution.

One morning I went to my primary school, escorted by the maid. I walked like someone being led off to prison. In my hand was a copybook,* in my eyes a look of dejection, in my heart a longing for anarchy. The cold air stung my half-naked legs below my shorts. We found the school closed, with the janitor saying in a stentorian voice, "Because of the demonstrations there will again be no school today."

A wave of joy flowed over me and swept me to the shores of happiness.

From the depths of my heart I prayed to God that the revolution might last forever.

NAGUIB MAHFOUZ
Translated by Denys Johnson-Davies

My Brother

His hair was light-colored
He went to bed early
And woke up early
One day he quietly went away
Just like he arrived—quietly
He was my brother

MOHAMMED AFIF HUSSAINI
Translated by Aziz Shihab

*copybook—blank notebook for school lessons

Dust

Imagine: only the dust
came along with me,
I had no other companion.
Came with me to kindergarten,
rumpled my hair
on the warmest days.

Imagine who came along with me
and everyone else had another companion.
When winter spreads terrible nets,
    when the clouds
devour their prey,
imagine who came with me
and how much
I wanted another companion.

The pine cones rustled
and I ached to be alone with the wind.
Nights I dreamed in a fever
about houses wet with love.
Imagine how unfair
that the dust
was my only companion.

On the days of the hot wind, I'd sail away
to the city of the leviathans,
full of a wild delight.
I'd never come back, not as long as I lived.

But when I came back,
I was like a raven despised

by his cousins the ravens.
I had no companion at all,
only the dust
came along with me.

DAHLIA RAVIKOVITCH
Translated by Chana Bloch

Rice Paradise

My grandmother wouldn't let us leave rice on our plates.
Instead of telling us about hunger in India
and children with swollen bellies
who would have opened their mouths wide
for each grain,
she would drag all the leftovers to the centers of our plates
with a screeching fork and, nearly in tears,
tell how the uneaten rice would rise to the heavens
to complain to God.
Now she's dead and I imagine the joy of the encounter
between her false teeth and the angels with flaming swords
at the gates of rice paradise.
They spread, beneath her feet, a carpet of red rice
and the yellow rice sun beats down on the lovely garden
of little white grains.
My grandmother spreads olive oil on their skins
and slips them one by one into the cosmic pots
of God's kitchen. Grandma, I feel like telling her,
rice is a seashell that shrunk, and like it
you rose from the sea.
The water of my life.

RONNY SOMECK
Translated by Vivian Eden

Beautiful Pattern from the Other Side, Tova Reznicek

Sumi's Infinity

Sumi said,
"I got a high score today—
710, 200, millions, infinity! Infinity, Dad!"
    "You mean infinity
    like the geese outside our window?"
"Yes, infinity like our window."
    (Infinity with a center or
    A hole, or no holes at all.
    Like a wall with a door.)
"Like music, Dad. Like that record,
Lucy in the Sky with Diamonds."
    (Like the threshing sound of cicadas
    in our elm and oak trees.)
"Do you remember what I said to Mom
when we were in the tunnel?—It's as long
as a bowl of yucky cereal . . . "

Oh, what a memory!
My son's memory is no burden,
Nor is mine any longer:
It's a ride through time,
A hike into infinity.
Memory, infinity
and time.

"I shielded myself from time
with the shadow of its wings,
so my eye sees time
but time sees me not.

If the days were asked
about me
They would not know
my name,
And about my
abode
They would not know
where I am."

MANSOUR AJAMI

13

History Class

In Mrs. Diaz's class
we would underline the text
while she read from the book
about the great kings that ruled India.

I spent the class
doodling in the margins,
coloring in the temples and mosques,
drawing mustaches and spectacles on the faces of dead kings.

In Mrs. Shenoy's geography class
we learned that a triangular chunk of land
broke off from Gondwananland,
floated up north
and collided with Asia.
The Himalayas crumpled upwards with the impact.

Years later
visiting a crumbling mosque outside Delhi,
doodles and drawings
floated up
from the underside of memory.

REZA SHIRAZI

Optimistic Man

as a child he never plucked the wings off flies
he didn't tie tin cans to cats' tails
or lock beetles in matchboxes
or stomp anthills
he grew up
and all those things were done to him
I was at his bedside when he died
he said read me a poem
about the sun and the sea
about nuclear reactors and satellites
about the greatness of humanity

NAZIM HIKMET
Translated by Randy Blasing and Mutlu Konuk

a childhood of moving streetlights,
changing eyes as the night's color shifted moods,
as belonging became deaf, as my mind accompanied
the sailboats across earth's heart while longing for a
corner in my grandfather's blood, while waiting
for the suitcase to retire,
the olive groves to expand...   expand

NATHALIE HANDAL

Cemetery from the East, Thuraya al-Baqsami

In the Mid-Thirties

In the mid-thirties
my uncle Zelig came from America
and took me and my mother
to a café on the beach of Tel Aviv, where
we ate something delightfully sweet.
Long years later I found out

it was the richest ice cream.
A band played, and mother laughed
when my uncle invited her to dance
the tango, as I found out long years later
with a few more facts,
for instance, that my father had been out of work
and the owner of the house where
we rented half a flat
was planning to throw us out
because we had not paid the rent
and those funny people, the *Yekkes*,*
who came to live in our neighborhood
were running away from Hitler—
we used to sing about him near to a lamp-post:
"One, two, three
Hitler came from Germany,
Where can he be found today?
The devils snatched him right away."
Who could have known then
that they didn't take him,
that he would live for ten more years.

I knew nothing of this
and yet I longed to stay there on the beach,
wanted mother to go on dancing, and for me—another ice cream
and that the setting sun would not put on its pink pajamas
and go to sleep on time

ARYEH SIVAN
Translated by the author and Arnold J. Band

*Yekkes—a nickname for Jews born in Germany who immigrated to Palestine in the 1930s

Watermelon Tales

January. Snow. For days I have craved
        watermelons, wanted
    to freckle the ground with seeds,
to perform a ritual:
        Noon time, an early
    summer Sunday, the village
chief faces north, spits seven mouthfuls,
        fingers a circle
    around a galaxy of seeds.

        ♦ ♦ ♦

Maimoon the Bedouin visited in
        summer, always with
    a gift: a pick-up truck load
of watermelons. "Something for
        the children," he explained.
    Neighbors brought wheelbarrows to
fetch their share. Our chickens ate the rest.

        ♦ ♦ ♦

        His right ear pricked up
    close, my father taps on a
watermelon, strokes as though it were
        a thigh. A light slap.
    "If it doesn't sound like your hands
clapping at a wedding, it's not yours."

        ♦ ♦ ♦

        Men shake the chief's hand,
    children kiss it. Everyone files
behind him when he walks back. No one
        talks until the tomb

        of the local saint. The rich
place coin sacks at his feet, the poor leave
        cups of melon seeds.

        ♦ ♦ ♦

        Maimoon also brought us meat,
gazelles he rammed with his truck.
        His daughter, Selima,
    said he once swerved off the road
suddenly, drove for an hour until
he spotted six. He hadn't
        hit any when the truck ran out
of gas. Thirty yards away the gazelles
        stood panting, and he
    ran to catch one with bare hands.

        ♦ ♦ ♦

Two choices, my father's doctor tells us:
        transplant or six months
    of pain. Outside the office,
I point to a fruit stall, the seller
        waving off flies with
    a feather fan. My father
strokes, slaps, and when I lift the melon
        to my shoulder says
"Eleven years in America
and you carry a watermelon
        like a peasant!"

        ♦ ♦ ♦

        Uncle Abdallah buries
a watermelon underneath the

approach of the waves—
"Like a refrigerator
down there." It's July, a picnic at
               Tokara Beach. We're
          kicking a ball when
my brother trips hard on the hole. He's
               told to eat what he'd
          broken too soon. I watched him
swallow pulp, seed, salt, and sand.

                    ♦ ♦ ♦

          Her shadow twice her
     height, the village sorceress
walks to where the chief spat. She reveals
               size of the harvest,
          chance of drought, whose sons will wed
whose daughters, and names of elders whose
               ailments will not cease.

                    ♦ ♦ ♦

          Selima told the gazelle
story sitting in a tub. With soap,
          my mother scrubbed the girl's scalp,
tossing handfuls of foam against
               the white tile. She then
          poured kerosene on Selima's
hair, rubbed till lice slid down her face,
               combed till the tines
          filled with the dead.

                    ♦ ♦ ♦

Selima married. My mother sent her
               a silver anklet,
          a green silk shawl, and decided
against an ivory comb. My father paid
               the sheikh to perform
          the wedding. A week later
at his door, the sheikh found three water-
               melons and a gazelle-
          skin prayer rug, a tire mark
across the spot where he would have rested his
               head in prostration.

                    ♦ ♦ ♦

          I cut the melon we bought
into cubes, strawberry red. But they were
               dry, almost bitter.
          After the third taste, my father
dropped his fork. He gazed at the window
               for a while, and spent
          the rest of his day in bed.

KHALED MATTAWA

Mr. Ahmet's Shoes

He'd spare his shoes and wouldn't walk in them
Every evening he'd clean them for the next day

He'd knock at their bottoms and listen to the sound
He'd say this is pure French leather

His shoes had a special brush and cloth
He'd always keep them clean inside and out

Every evening as soon as he got home he'd put on his slippers
His only concern in life was his shoes

He'd set out with a *bismillah** and walk on asphalt roads
He knew that this shoe nation would rot in snow waters

The shoes had their place reserved next to the door
Poor Mr. Ahmet would put them side by side

He'd say, "These shoes will last for so many more years."
He'd say so but unfortunately his life did not last that long

They did not throw his shoes away
Nor did they sell them to anyone as the shoes had great memories.

KEMALETTIN TUĞCU
Translated by Yusuf Eradam

*bismillah—"in the name of Allah" (God)

I Remember My Father's Hands

because they were large, and square,
fingers chunky, black hair like wire

because they fingered worry beads over and over
(that muted clicking, that constant motion, that secular prayer)

because they ripped bread with quiet purpose,
dipped fresh green oil like a birthright

because after his mother's funeral they raised a tea cup,
set it down untouched, uncontrollably trembling

because when they trimmed hedges, pruned roses,
their tenderness caught my breath with jealousy

because once when I was a child they cupped my face,
dry and warm, flesh full and calloused, for a long moment

because over his wife's still form they faltered
great mute helpless beasts

because when his own lungs filled and sank they reached out
for the first time pleading

because when I look at my hands
his own speak back

LISA SUHAIR MAJAJ

In the Garden, Linda Dalal Sawaya

My Uncle Wore a Rose on His Lapel

And as if it were alive he would water it every day.
To let the water on his dark flesh vaporize
He would button down his shirt with rascally strong words:

A florist he was who would not kill lice on a leaf.
A photographer who touched up the photographs of war.
A storyteller who came home smiling every night.
Auburn he was—his children resembled his wife.
His tallness protected him from the cold.
A greengrocer who never ate his own tomatoes.
A merchant who knew no cushions but matting.
Religious—he would not drink *raki** during *edhan.***
The glasses he wore made his eyes seem larger.
Wanderer he was who trod the cobblestones of Izmir.
A fisherman whose hands became calloused by water.
A nicotine addict whose long cigarette curled.
A diplomat who attended cocktail parties with his fancy trousers on.
An investor who worked overtime to feed his family.

My uncle wore a rose on his lapel.
Had he seen you he would have cried with joy.

ALI CENGIZKAN
Translated by Asalet Erten

*raki—Turkish alcoholic drink made from aromatic anise
**edhan—call for prayer in Turkey for the Muslims

The Neighbors Think I Am a Star

— I am born of a basil plant. I have run in an antique dish.

— There is a nail in my shoes. A thorn in my beard. These are my possessions.

— I open the umbrella and the bottles. I ski on all geography.

— I summer in the neck of a giraffe.

— I am stiff from blasting winds.

— I swallow a seal and pods of hot pepper on an empty stomach.

— I am planted in a basket and I go to weddings.

— I eat the prepositions and the exclamation mark.

— I fix the train. Lawsuits and suitcases fall on my backbone.

— I glitter but I am neither gold nor the Pope.

— I sneeze and, lo, buttons and barrels topple.

— Stones do not bear children.

— The ant is an olive. A lady. A carpet. A yacht with a ribbon. Two and a half piasters.*

— The bird is a piano.

— I lost** in the municipal election and so my shoulder was bruised. I read the newspaper upside down.

— I light the hearth with scissors.

— The fig tree is beloved of the Kurds. The plum tree is the buttons of a Cardinal.

— I visit in my pajamas. The neighbors think I am a star.

— I feel my way with pins like a tailor.

— I have lost my wallet. In it I had a lamb, a snail, and five piasters.

— A fire broke out in my eyes. The tenants and the soldiers ran away.

— I left the book open. Enemies, tigers, and judges fell into it.

— I swim in a jar.

— I have a collection of pigs, butterflies, and fried potatoes.

— My paternal uncle snores. He has a lot of dreams. He loves his wife like an onion.

— My maternal uncle is a heavy drinker. He tramples on scorpions with his boots.

— I place my heart on the table like a watch.

— My head hit the ceiling, so the electricity went out.

— I spend the evening at the window. I talk with Miss A and Mrs. Z.

— A duck lives on the first floor. A fly on the second. A chick pea on the third. We live on the top floor.

— *Sabbù*[†] is a gold finch; *ḥassun*[†] not a man.

— I pinch my fiancée. Blood shoots from her. She gives it to the Red Cross.

— I create light with a lighter. I spy. I write fire on a bear's skin. I snatch its moustache.

— Frogs do not slumber. They stay up all night playing cards.

— I stand alone with the *hamza*[††] on top of the *alif*.[††]

SHAWQI ABI SHAQRA

Translated by Mansour Ajami

---

*piasters—coins

** "lost" in Arabic also means "I fell down," indicating a loss.

[†]*Sabbù* is the diminutive of *sab'* (a beast). It is a man's nickname; so is *ḥassun*, diminutive of Hassan and a nickname.

[††]*Hamza* is a glottal stop and the first letter of the Arabic alphabet. It cannot stand on its own at the beginning of a word. The *alif* (a vertical stroke written like the number one, "1") acts as a seat for the *hamza*. Hamza on top of the *alif* thus forms the first letter of the alphabet.

Growing
after Pablo Neruda's "Walking Around"

It so happens I am happy to be a daughter
and it happens that I dance into dinner parties and Arabic concerts
dressed up, polished, like a pearl in
the tender hands of a diver
sliding on my path in a garden of olive trees and jasmine.

The scent of my mother sends me to a green orchard.
My only wish is to grow like seeds or trees,
my only wish is to see no more death, no poverty,
no more maimed, no drunks, no drugs.

It so happens that I am delighted
by my father's victories and his pride
and his brown eyes and his bald head.
It so happens he is happy to be my father.

And I'd feel lucky
if I attended my parents' 50th wedding anniversary
or conceived a child with dark curly hair.
It would be wonderful to free my country with honest talk
planting orange trees until I died of happiness.

I want to go on following the moon—
bright, silvery, secure with the light
casting jasmine into the bloody streets of Jerusalem,
blossoming every day.

I don't want to fall in a grave,
restless underneath the weight, a martyr for nothing,
dried-up, battling against the lies.

That's why my mother, when she greets me
with her outstretched arms gives me the moon,
and she runs through the arching streets of Gaza,
and stops to stare at the white minarets of the mosques,
planting seeds of green fruit.

And my father leads me to the Golden Dome of the Rock
into debates about survival
into gatherings where friends speak of the good past,
into houses that remind me of home
into a sunny shelter cradled like a baby nursing
from a beloved breast.

There are starving children, and homeless people
hovering in the polluted air that I hate.
There are malignant cysts
that should disappear from bodies and skin.
There are soldiers all over, and machine-guns, and tear gas.

I climb slowly with my moon, my roots, my dome,
remembering my parents,
I hike up, through the sloping hills and green orchards,
and gardens of olive trees smelling of jasmine
in which little white petals are growing.

DEEMA SHEHABI KHORSHEED

Via Capelli, Helen Zughaib

Childhood. 1948

Do you remember our childhood?
There was the brook, there was the palm tree;
It was bountiful and the dates delicious,
Soft and you by my side.
Early mornings were red—the morning star was bright
And gone now.
Here is white milk for you, though, warm and foamy,
Drink it, dear, take the little kids and the big goatie goats
To the riverside to graze, while we bathe a while.
No! How can I forget all this? No!
You were a child and I was a child. You dripped honey
And I collected dates.
The palm was lovely on the mound in the sand.
It loved our love, and there under the tender care of its shade,
It grew.
Little lovely tree, it stood there—still, dignified, unafraid
Little palm.

Alas, alas, it has all been drowned.
We saw it going down, going down
While we were going away.
Oh God, forgive those who drowned it!
God forgive us, those who have forsaken it.

Hamza El Din

Legend I, Suad al-Attar

"THE WORLD IS A GLASS YOU DRINK FROM"

Attention

Those who come by me passing
I will remember them
and those who come heavy and overbearing
I will forget

That's why
when the air erupts between mountains
we always describe the wind
and forget the rocks

SAADI YOUSSEF
Translated by Khaled Mattawa

As I traveled from the city
toward the country
old age fell off my shoulders.

SALAH FA'IQ
Translated by Patricia Alanah Byrne
and Salma Khadra Jayyusi

Red pomegranate, juicy
swollen with seeds and memories
falls with the moon
into the hands of naked children

TAHAR BEN JELLOUN
Translated by Nadia Benabid

Al Nada*

An
epic
of
flowers
told
as
drops
of
dew
.
Stories
I
tell
to
the
fingerprints
:
left
to
mark
a
dream
of
loneliness
.

A flower is never alone.

NADINE RACHID LAURE TOUMA

*Al Nada—"dew" in Arabic

Untitled, Sawsan Amer

Letters

When the earth was still covered with water,
someone drew his name there, as a child would,
in block letters. Long afterward, when the earth
dried off, the letters were inscribed as if in rock,
as if from the age of an ancient king. Later,
there came the ones who overpowered the earth
with their shoes, and after them dogs with their claws,
and the wild grasses. And then the falling leaves served
as a mantle, tenderly cast down over the faces
of the dead while the good earth caused the bones
of the dead ones to feel at ease. And a long,
a fruitful sleep fell upon them. He who looks now
will see only the bare rudiments of a name,
he will remember that something heroic happened here.
And these will be sufficient for him because he
is only a traveler or because these are signs enough
for the wandering poet.

MOSHE DOR
Translated by Myra Sklarew

Jisr el-Qadi*

In a place of wind and clay pitchers,
in a place of a bridge and a road,
in a place as fresh as water,
in a place where a foot touches
softly as a blossom on a stream,
in a place where a bird's passing
is only a pressure by your cheek,
in a place which means nothing,
in a place which stays precise as childhood,
in a place transformed by absent moons,
in a place of two hands, a potter's wheel and some clay,
in a place where you can be still,
in a place where the world is a glass you drink from.

NADIA TUÉNI
Translated by Samuel Hazo

The Kingdom

His kingdom is an ancient lamp,
a walking stick,
a water bag.

At the door of his dwelling
the sun slants
and the stars are resting.

FUAD RIFKA
Translated by Aziz Shihab

*Jisr el-Qadi—a town in Lebanon

When the Good Earth Doesn't Accept You

The tree was young,
the earth red and rich,
the air invisible.
My back felt comfortable
against the rugged trunk,
and my bottom pressed against the soil.
When a farmer came along, a happy farmer—
with a yoke upon his shoulder.
"The cows are tired and so am I," said he,
and sat next to me.
He smelled of earth and green grass.
He resembled the rocks . . .
the trees felt comfortable in his presence.
A few drops of sweat fell from his forehead.
He looked gracious as the good earth absorbed them.
That moment I experienced misery,
as if my tears had never been accepted by that earth . . .
and I loved that earth.

Daoud Boulos

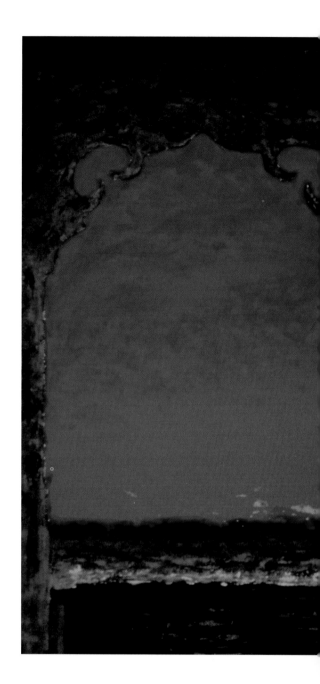

Birth, Balqees Fakhro

The Train of the Stars

The night is a train that passes,
Up on my house I watch it
Its eyes smile to me.

The night is a train that passes,
Carrying moons and stars
Clouds, flowers,
Seas and rivers that run.
The night is a train that passes.

The night is a train that passes,
I wish, oh, how I wish!
I could take it one day:
It would take me away,
To see where it's going.
Oh, where's that train going?

ABDUL-RAHEEM SALEH AL-RAHEEM
Translated by Adil Saleh Abid

Evening

They are breaking walnuts, I look;
They are breaking the wall of the nut.
The nut comes out . . .
Then the children get busy with their games.

I too pick a walnut
Amongst the many walnuts.
The sea comes out of my walnut.
I set sail.

I am sailing in the wall of that nut,
Away from the gameless games of my childhood.
One evening in that child game
Away from the sea of sadness written on my forehead.

Özdemir Asaf
Translated by Yusuf Eradam

The Flamingo

The enclosed, self-possessed one spreads his wings across the lake, beak
    pointing downwards, eyes searching out the bright movement of
    water serpents and green flies.
How he wishes for his victims to be sad when he pounces on them from
    above, but they are mute and merry,
merry in the mirthful water:
This is what makes him sad,
what saddens the mute flamingo, as he continues to pounce,
generation after generation, upon the mute gaiety of the water.

SALEEM BARAKAT
Translated by Lena Jayyusi and Naomi Shihab Nye

Class Pictures

In the last week of school
There's a camera in class, and smiles
(the teacher's in the center, wearing flowers.)
Gideon is next to Yael,
They're a couple.
Ruth's eyes are closed, she's dreaming.
And I'm not in the picture.
I had the measles.

On the last day of school
There's a camera in the yard, and smiles.
(the teacher's next to me, wearing flowers.)

And Gideon and Yael
Are no longer a couple.
Yael closes her eyes, she's dreaming.
Ruth isn't in the picture.
She had the measles.

In the class picture,
In the yard, or in the building,
Someone is always missing.

SHLOMIT COHEN-ASSIF
Translated by Nelly Segal

The Lost Mirage

O mirage, do you not complain of weariness at noonday heat?
You appear like water on the vast horizon
goading the traveller to lengthen out his way,
You seem like one of the streams of paradise, nourishing life with its virtue,
like the mist from the light of a censer* that kindles perfumes at the altar.
In the waste you are like a lost dream in the eyes of a girl,
ever moving, as if in love with the wilderness.
Have mercy on those a-thirst in vacancy, the caravan comes near to agony.
Always you waken longing when the caravan is lost and the rain clouds are
     sparse.
You whose essence baffles man—you are the mystery of all the ages.
Did you come down from the clouds above, rise from the earth below?
Are you the dream of the waterless desert when noon heat blazes upon
     the hills?
We are alike, lost in this life, and both our fates are dark.
But I, unlike you, you deceiver of travellers,
am lost in my own country, and among my friends!

AHMAD MUHAMMAD AL KHALIFA

Translated by Christopher Nouryeh and John Heath-Stubbs

*censer—a vessel for burning incense

Horizon of Peace, Helen Khal

River, Fatima Hassan El-Farouj

Night in Hamdan

We in Hamdan say:
Sleep when the date palms sleep
When the stars rise over a village
the lights of huts are extinguished
the mosque and the old house
It is the long sleep
under the whispers of faded palm fronds: the long death
This is Hamdan . . .
tuberculosis and date palms
In Hamdan we only listen to what we say
our night, the date palms, esparto grass
and the old river
where lemon leaves on the water float
They are green like water like your eyes I say
You from whose eyes we expect spring
How can a friend forget you?
I will meet you
when the setting of the stars covers Hamdan
when heavy night settles on the city

♦ ♦ ♦

and together we in the depths of Baghdad will roam
when the setting of the stars covers Hamdan

SAADI YOUSSEF
Translated by Khaled Mattawa

Sea

I'm not jealous of the pond
that's sleeping so quietly
in the middle of the forest.
I'm the sea,
I'm not afraid of the storm.
The sea's dream is always
turbulence.
If I don't have waves and storms,
I won't be the sea anymore.
I'll be the pond—
and stinking.

SHAFEE'E KADKANI
Translated by Ali Maza-heri

Winter, Akbar Nikonpour

A Voiced Lament

Who's sprinkled salt on our children's milk
Who's muddied our waters
Hey, who goes there?

Are we living a fairy-tale, which century is this
Whence can the poison have seeped
Into our apple, onto our comb?

The light of day comes to our room unbidden
Wakes us and takes us away, forces
A pick-axe, a pen into our hands
The wagonloads go past, go past
Pushed into harness, we climb the slope

We pluck night from the forty thieves
Sing it a lullaby in our arms
Should not its arms enfold our sleep
Who is rocking whom?

They are walking the dead away
Mindful of proper ceremony
Is that the wind, is someone blowing
The living are in their lockers
Then who is it whose breath
Ruffles these well-kept files
Hey, who goes there?

GÜLTEN AKIN
Translated by Nermin Menemencioğlu

45

Sand

the handful of sand that I'm holding means
I'm holding in my hand
the bottom storms,
the tossed seaweed
a big fish descending deeper silently.

SALIH BOLAT
Translated by Asalet Erten

A Poem of Bliss

We are placed on a wedding cake
like the two dolls, bride and groom.
When the knife strikes
we'll try to stay on the same slice.

RONNY SOMECK
Translated by Yair Mazor

Love

Love is:
Five o'clock in the evening.
Exactly five
in two hearts at least.

SAÂD SARHAN
Translated by Assef al-Jundi

Borrowed Tongue

Maybe I'm a fool
holding two threads,
one black, one white,
waiting for dawn
to tell them apart.
But I'm only practicing
my religion which
I neither borrowed
nor stole.
Maybe I'm a fool
thinking of a better answer
than the transplant patient
who said *I'm sorry
someone had to die.*

No, I haven't outgrown
my tongue. It's a coat
your mother gives you,
crimson or cobalt blue,
satin inside, the collar
wide enough to cover
your whole neck.
All winter you wear it
then spring comes
but never goes.

That's Arabic to me.
I wear a white shirt now—
thin gray stripes,
top button gone—
and it fits.

KHALED MATTAWA

47

Two Arabian Horses, Ovissi

The Path of Affection

Along the amazing road drawn from the throat of recent dates . . .
Along the amazing road drawn from my old Jerusalem,
And despite the hybrid signs, shops, and cemeteries,
My fragmented self drew together to meet the kin of New Haifa. . . .
The earth remained unchanged as of old,
With all its mortgaged trees dotting the hills,
And all the green clouds and the plants
Fertilized with fresh fertilizers,
And efficient sprinklers. . . .
In the earth there was an apology for my father's wounds,
And all along the bridges was my Arab countenance,
In the tall poplars,
In the trains and windows,
In the smoke rings.
Everything is Arab despite the change of tongue,
Despite the trucks, the cars, and the car lights. . . .
All the poplars and my ancestor's solemn orchards
Were, I swear, smiling at me with Arab affection.
Despite all that had been eliminated and coordinated and the "modern" sounds . . .
Despite the seas of light and technology. . . .
O my grandparents, the rich soil was bright with Arab reserve,
And it sang out, believe me, with affection.

LAYLA 'ALLUSH
Translated by Abdelwahab M. Elmessiri

from Ziad's* Little Moons

When darkness prevails
    I go to bed
Where does the moon** sleep?

◆ ◆ ◆

A moon roaming everywhere
Walking through the clouds
A stick in one hand, lantern in the other.
If he sees a bed on which a child lies,
He spends the night at the window
    in guard
So that the child's sleep
Will not be disturbed.

◆ ◆ ◆

When I missed the moon
I drew him in my book.
At night he did not appear.
Dad looked at the sky
But could not see the moon.
Mom gazed at the clouds
But could not see the moon.
I laughed in secret.
I didn't tell them
I hid him in my book.

◆ ◆ ◆

The white-faced moon
Was surprised by darkness

He paled and ran to me
Begged me to stay with him
Till the darkness went away.
Mom wouldn't let me out
So I stayed at my window
To entertain him
And shyly, he came nearer.

◆ ◆ ◆

Grandfather finished his story.
My warm bed felt perfect
And sleep was wonderful.
But nobody understands what I mean:
Moon is alone in that cold night.
I closed my eyes pretending to sleep.
My mother carried me to bed.
She kissed me and left me by myself.
Moon was outside alone in that cold.
He rubbed his face, begging at my window
I said, You will not stay out in that cold
Come inside.
Nobody sees us.
You are my brother.
You will sleep beside me.

MAMDOUH ADWAN
Translated by the author

*Ziad is the name of the author's son.
**The moon in Arabic culture is considered male and the sun female.

Silent Night, Ora Eitan

Awakening

Darkness slowly lifts
the yawning street
shakes off the remnants of long sleep

garbage still heaped at the corners
the shops still closed
and little trees search for their reflections
in the shining window panes.

Now the houses begin to show some movement
a window opens here
a balcony there as a lovely shadow
emerges with the morning light
A little while, then quickly
the earth goes crazy
a bus appears,
then another,
then another,
and people rush forth in every street and alley.

SAMI MAHDI
Translated by May Jayyusi

Village de Chtouka, Chaibia Tallal

Poverty Line

As if you could stretch a line and say: below it, poverty.
Here's the bread blackened with cheap make-up
and the olives in a small plate on the tablecloth.

In the air, doves flew a soaring salute
to the kerosene vendor's ringing bell on his cart
and the sound of rubber boots landed on the muddy ground.

I was a kid, in a house they called a shanty,
in a neighborhood called a transit camp.
The only line I saw was the horizon and under it everything
looked poor.

RONNY SOMECK

Translated by Ammiel Alcalay

Snapshots

Amman is softer than/ the skin of goats
         —A BEDOUIN POET

In the blink of an eye
flesh and cement
take over its ancient hills.

No river wets its throat.
The wisps of grass
turn yellow
under the first footfalls
of summer,

and the few birds
that come by
look puzzled, pained
like migrant workers.

♦ ♦ ♦

Up and down the steep hills
cars, humped like camels,
issue their pleas.

In the minaret
God gets used
to loudspeakers.

SHARIF S. ELMUSA

Song of the Season of the Turnip Cooking

When Yima Yister used to recall her dead daughter Kmerah
Yima Makhah would recall her dead son Haroun
And all the neighbor-women would recall the troubles of their days
Leaving the making of the bread in the *ferran**
The cooking of the sweet turnips, the weaving of blankets
Yima Z'herah, Yima Se'edah, Yima Kh'ninah,
Then as at a holy-day service, there would rise a great glee of weeping
And we children used to convulse with laughter
Actually choking from so much laughter,
And scoffing and teasing.
When Yima Yister used to recall her dead daughter Kmerah
Yima Makhah Yima Z'herah Yima Se'edah
Would leave their day's chores
The baking of the bread in the *ferran** and the cooking of the sweet turnips
And the making of the blankets
And we children would wriggle with laughter really convulsed with laughter
And the smell of the turnips would rise and swell and catch in our clothes and chase us
But sometimes when we calmed down we would steal away from the weeping
And go to a little hut we'd made at the edge of the quarter, and there we'd make
beds for ourselves and food for ourselves, there we made little women for ourselves
And we called them: My Louisa and my Yakot and my Shabah.
There we built big houses inside a little hut
And there we made peace for ourselves inside ourselves.

Erez Biton
Translated by Richard Flantz

*ferran—an oven

Impossible Dream, Leila Shawa

One Day Vacation

I exempt Monday morning from music
I exempt the radio
I exempt my hand from all its chores
I exempt my ribs
I exempt the day from all earthly cares
I stifle all pain
I exempt silence from all declarations
I exempt the door from the key
and I set the winds free.

MUHAMMAD AL-QAISI
Translated by May Jayyusi and Jeremy Reed

Taste of Saltiness

Cities are God's letters to us
No one letter is like another

My bags long for travel
And my spirit shuts its doors here

Ports and lakes
A fishing hook
And dense faces

They have the taste of saltiness
And their hands hold countless shells.

DHABIYA KHAMIS
Translated by Assef al-Jundi

A Saddle & The World

In Palestine, an old disheveled street,
a wall of tiny shops, where grass grows between crumpled stone,
I stand and watch in the shadow of the wall.
Pots and tin pans and brooms and woven straw mats,
even handmade saddles, spill into the narrow street.
Heavy saddles, covered with burlap, to fit horses,
mules, donkeys, sewn by someone who knows saddles.
A woman in a *thobe*—a long black dress,
hand-embroidered with red cross-stitching on chest and sides—
pokes around the saddles.
Bending down, she touches, pats, caresses,
like a woman buying cloth.
Finally she lifts her head, then do-si-dos
toward the bald man who owns the shop
and asks the price of the saddle she likes best.
But the price isn't set in stone and will change, like the weather,
if you have some smarts at this haggling game.
Like fencing, you dance with agile steps around each other,
touch with the point of your foil, but never wound.
He says, she says. Words fly, as conductor-hands
sweep the air for emphasis. The woman nods,
and a corner of her mouth lifts. She fingers the coins
inside the slit in her belt.
"Sold! To the woman in embroidered dress!" the auctioneer would call out
if she lived in Texas. Or Oklahoma. Or even New York.
But in Palestine where she lives, a thousand women in embroidered dresses
would stand to claim the prize.
I, in the uniform of my faded American jeans,
ask the woman a foolish question,

"How will you take this saddle home?"
The woman's face cracks open, a smile spills out.
Squatting, she picks up the saddle, an Olympian heavyweight champion,
she hoists the saddle in the air, then lowers it onto her head.
She stands tall, this Palestinian Yoga-woman, her head not merely holding
      a saddle,
But the world.

MAY MANSOOR MUNN

Feast in the Desert, Fahrelnissa Zeid

Two Hands On the Water

A face reigned on the water
      but did not sleep
It was the face of pain.

two hands that grew green with prayer
     were
          the hands of the poor.

A face floated on the water
      but did not sleep
It was the face of God.

The guardian of the morning wanders
        between the Khalili Bazaar
     and the Mosque of Husain
He stretches two hands:
     one bargaining with the Khalili Bazaar
     playing with the Khalili Bazaar
     stringing bracelets on the wrists
        of the Khalili Bazaar

and the other
     picking autumn flies
     off the children's faces
        in the Grand Mosque of Husain

ZUHUR DIXON

Translated by Patricia Alanah Byrne and Salma Khadra Jayyusi

The Crusader Man

The Crusader man paid the Land a visit
and that was
around
so and so many
years back.

The Crusader man did the country
in this
or that many days.

The Crusader became the landlord.
An enemy with holdings.
Full of trust,
sword-bearing, armor-wearing, with a coat of mail.

Kind of a jumpy guy, the Crusader man.

The Land is a witness,
she sees it from
the way he laid his
place out,
from the fact

that he never did make himself a home.
From the way he'd attack
and cut himself off on the mountaintops.

SHELLEY ELKAYAM
Translated by Ammiel Alcalay

A Dream

When he surrendered his eyes to the dream, this lad,
The evening star entered his house, trembling,
The wood of his bed turned into a ship for him,
The cosmos turned to an oyster in his hands.

MUHAMMAD AL-GHUZZI
Translated by May Jayyusi and John Heath-Stubbs

Bethlehem

Secrets live in the space between our footsteps.
The words of my grandfather echoed in my dreams,
as the years kept his beads and town.
I saw Bethlehem, all in dust, an empty town
with a torn piece of newspaper lost in its narrow streets.
Where could everyone be? Graffitis and stones answered.
And where was the real Bethlehem—the one my grandfather came from?
Handkerchiefs dried the pain from my hands. Olive trees and tears continued to remember.
I walked the town until I reached an old Arab man dressed in a white robe.
I stopped him and asked, "Aren't you the man I saw in my grandfather's stories?"
He looked at me and left. I followed him—asked him why he left? He continued walking.
I stopped, turned around and realized he had left me the secrets in the space between his
    footsteps.

NATHALIE HANDAL

Table

A man filled with the gladness of living
Put his keys on the table,
Put flowers in a copper bowl there.
He put his eggs and milk on the table.
He put there the light that came in through the window,
Sound of a bicycle, sound of a spinning wheel.
The softness of bread and weather he put there.
On the table the man put
Things that happened in his mind.
What he wanted to do in life.
He put that there.
Those he loved, those he didn't love,
The man put them on the table too.
Three times three make nine:
The man put nine on the table.
He was next to the window next to the sky;
He reached out and placed on the table endlessness.
So many days he had wanted to drink a beer!
He put on the table the pouring of that beer.
He placed there his sleep and his wakefulness;
His hunger and his fullness he placed there.

Now that's what I call a table!
It didn't complain at all about the load.
It wobbled once or twice, then stood firm.
The man kept piling things on.

EDIP CANSEVER
Translated by Richard Tillinghast

The Strange Tale

We laughed at the past.
Tomorrow the future will be laughing
    at us.
This is the world, a tale spun
    by some great magician.
The living perform the marvelous play
as if they were already dead.

The stage is sad
    with its curtain of mist.
And beyond the curtain,
the audience of the future watches us, laughing.
They don't see how the script
is falling into their own hands.

ABU-L-QASIM AL-SHABBI

Translated by Lena Jayyusi and Naomi Shihab Nye

Prison 126, Inji Efflatoun

Unoccupied Chairs

Squares following one another
  A square for your face by itself
  A square for faces of passing friends
  A square for silence...by itself
  A square for the clamor of sudden emotions

A square for rendezvous cloaked with parting
A square for your affection and loathing...together

A square for me...with you and without you.

    The square is mine!

DHABIYA KHAMIS
Translated by Assef al-Jundi

Every Day Is April 23rd, Reha Yalnizcik

"pick a sky and name it"

rice haikus

we are women simple
sugar our morning tea
eat rice at all meals

we of simple land
kept the sugar in one sack
rice in another

lived off the brown earth
gave figs to *fidayeen**
olives and almonds

when they raided homes
they poured sugar into rice
to ruin them both

with eyelashes and
teeth we tried to sort it out
small grain from small grain

now we eat sweet rice
with our morning tea eat
meals of resistance

SUHEIR HAMMAD

In the Name of God, Nidal Kamal Tabbal

*fidayeen—popular name for freedom fighters

Through galaxies of stars and planets
I sail
in vessels of salt and crystal
navigating across black bareness
and deserts within. In
the harbor of dreams I find
myself. The world
is reduced to the size of a toy.
A blind singer begins with a song
I hover in the dark of the night
I fall in love
with All
now blind.

Tonight, I am born.
Tonight, I die.
Greetings to all the living
        and all the dead.

MONA SA'UDI
Translated by Kamal Boullata

Pink

The night has come,
Pink's job is done.
She was the dawn, and the pink sun.
But now blue's time has come.
He'll be the moon,
He'll be the sky.
Pink sits and waits for sunrise,
Then she'll be the sun again,
She'll be the sky.
But sunrise won't last long.
When yellow comes
And spreads her color to the sun.
Pink sits and waits.
Pink sits and waits.

ZEYNEP BELER

Why Are We in Exile the Refugees Ask

Why do we die
In silence
And I had a house
And I had . . .
And here you are
Without a heart, without a voice
Wailing, and here you are
Why are we in exile?
We die
We die in silence
Why are we not crying?
On fire,
On thorns
We walked
And my people walked
Why are we Lord
Without a country, without love
We die
We die in terror
Why are we in exile
Why are we Lord?

ABDUL WAHAB AL-BAYATI
Translated by Abdullah al-Udhari

Arabic Council, Omar Bsoul

From the Diary of an Almost-Four-Year-Old

Tomorrow, the bandages
will come off. I wonder
will I see half an orange,
half an apple, half my
mother's face
with my one remaining eye?

I did not see the bullet
but felt its pain
exploding in my head.
His image did not
vanish, the soldier
with a big gun, unsteady
hands, and a look in
his eyes
I could not understand.

If I can see him so clearly
with my eyes closed,
it could be that inside our heads
we each have one spare set
of eyes
to make up for the ones we lose.

Next month, on my birthday,
I'll have a brand new glass eye,
maybe things will look round
and fat in the middle—
I've gazed through all my marbles,
they made the world look strange.

I hear a nine-month-old
has also lost an eye,
I wonder if my soldier
shot her too—a soldier
looking for little girls who
look him in the eye—
I'm old enough, almost four,
I've seen enough of life,
but she's just a baby
who didn't know any better.

Hanan Mikha'il 'Ashrawi

White Jacket

The white-wool knit jacket
With a decorative pin
Which my grandpa and grandma sent me from Kovel
When I was two
And it was sent to the communal storeroom*
And I never wore it, not even once,
My God,
Grandma and Grandpa were murdered there
A whole Jewry destroyed
And I searched throughout my life
For a white-wool knit jacket
Which my grandma knit for me and decorated
With a pin
And went to the post office and sent it
In a package which my grandpa had packed lovingly
A small white hand-knitted jacket
For a little girl of two
All my life
And cannot find it.

YEHUDIT KAFRI
Translated by Lami

*In communal Israeli settlements, kibbutzim, of the thirties, clothes for all the adults and children
were kept in and distributed from a central storeroom.

from *The Sound of Water's Footsteps*

I am from Kashan . . .
I am a Moslem
my Mecca is a red rose
my prayer-spread the stream, my holy clay the light
my prayer-rug the field
I do ablutions to the rhythm of the rain upon the windowpane
In my prayer runs the moon, runs the light
the particles of my prayer have turned translucent
upon the minaret of the cypress tree
I say my prayer in the mosque of grass
and follow the sitting and rising of the wave . . .

I saw many things upon the earth:
I saw a beggar who went from door to door
singing the larks' song
I saw a poet who addressed the lily of the valley as "lady" . . .
I saw a train carrying light
I saw a train carrying politics (and going so empty)
I saw a train carrying morning-glory seeds and canary songs
and a plane, through its window
a thousand feet high, one could see the earth:
one could see the hoopoe's crest
the butterfly's beauty-spots
the passage of a fly across the alley of loneliness
the luminous wish of a sparrow descending from a pine . . .

I hear the sound of gardens breathing
the sound of the darkness raining from a leaf
the light clearing its throat behind the tree . . .

Sometimes, like a stream pebble, my soul is washed clean and shines
I haven't seen two pine trees hate each other
I haven't seen a poplar sell its shadow
the elm tree gives its branch to the crow at no charge
wherever there is a leaf I rejoice . . .

SOHRAB SEPEHRI
Translated by Massud Farzan

The Tent, Faik Hassan

Sleep

Don't send me flowers
Send me a bird tree
With pigeons strolling
On its branches

Let the pigeons land on my pillow
To put me to sleep
Feathers on their backs
Lullaby on their beaks

Let them raise my bed high
And fly it up into heavens
And let me suddenly find myself
Among the stars

Don't send me flowers
Send me a bird tree
Those that touch my forehead
Should say "He has recovered."

ÜLKÜ TAMER
Translated by Yusuf Eradam

How can I escape this busy life
when it is the cloth of every day?

♦ ♦ ♦

I sleep for six or seven hours
during which my mind never quiets down
since I return to years past
which now do not exist
and see faces
I thought had left me forever.

♦ ♦ ♦

This is a strange city.
Every time I solve one problem
ten new ones appear on the horizon.

♦ ♦ ♦

Today I realize
that my spirit has rusted
to a degree
I shall not be able
to shine it again.

♦ ♦ ♦

If the past is spread behind me
and the future is spread before me,
in this there is the comfort
of my current struggle.

MAHMUD SHURAYH
Translated by Aziz Shihab

from *"For the Photographs of Constantine Manos"*

You, the child thinking in front of his home!
You will grow up one day.
You too will have a living room, your threshold will hold shoes
You too will have a house you clean with a broom.

If they ask you to take the picture of time
What would you take, the light, the stairs,
My granny with her walking stick, or the little girl on the stone
Or the stone, the texture of the wall, or the odor of the air?

ALI CENGIZKAN
Translated by Yusuf Eradam

Untitled, Kamel Brahim

But I Heard the Drops

My father had a reservoir
of tears.
They trickled down
unseen.
But I heard the drops
drip
from his voice
like drops
from a loosened tap.
For thirty years
I heard them.

SHARIF S. ELMUSA

from The Awakening

What happened
to the wood gatherer?
In old times he used to sing
like a bird on the shoulder of a mountain
early in the morning.
And today he doesn't speak,
he became mute
like a stone in a cave.
Who knows? Maybe he got tired.
When the river gets tired
it loves the flat lands
and the darkness of the sea.

FUAD RIFKA
Translated by Aziz Shihab

End of a Discussion With a Jailer

From the window of my small cell
I can see trees smiling at me,
Roofs filled with my people,
Windows weeping and praying for me.
From the window of my small cell
I can see your large cell.

SAMIH AL-QASIM
Translated by Abdullah al-Udhari

On the Way to the Wall

None of my business
I said
And left
Colors came running after me
Not my business

I passed fallen staircases
Did not concern me
Trumpets cracking
The street
Rain
On the street
And nothing
But it was none of my business

I arrived at the wall
I entered into it

Like this
I flung my feet in the air

LINA TIBI
Translated by Assef al-Jundi

Shadow and Walls, Mohamad M. Samara

Homeland

Anxious, anxious am I for a homeland,
The windows of my longing are open.
     How tired I am of moving around
     The walking stick of travel
               is nearly broken
So I take refuge in my dreams
I sing my songs
I travel in my imagination
to the shores of my homeland
Oh, how much I long for a homeland

BALKIS SALEEM ZAGHAL

Translated by Aziz Shihab

from *The Mailman*

Whether at dawn or in the middle of the night,
I've carried people news
—of other people, the world, and my country,
    of trees, the birds and the beasts—
        in the bag of my heart.

I've been a poet,
    which is a kind of mailman.
As a child, I wanted to be a mailman,
not via poetry or anything
but literally—a real mail carrier.
In geography books and Jules Verne's novels
my colored pencils drew a thousand different pictures
    of the same mailman—Nazim.
Here, I'm driving a dogsled
      over ice,
canned goods and mail packets
      glint in the Arctic twilight:
I'm crossing the Bering Strait.
Or here, under the shadow of heavy clouds on the steppe,
I'm handing out mail to soldiers and drinking kefir.*
Or here, on the humming asphalt of a big city,
I bring only good news
                and hope.
Or I'm in the desert, under the stars,
a little girl lies burning up with fever,
and there's a knock on the door at midnight:
"Mailman!"

kefir—a yogurt drink

The little girl opens her big blue eyes:
her father will come home from prison tomorrow.
I was the one who found that house in the snowstorm
and gave the neighbor girl the telegram.
As a child, I wanted to be a mailman.
But it's a difficult art in my Turkey.
In that beautiful country
    a mailman bears all manner of pain in telegrams
      and line on line of grief in letters.
As a child, I wanted to be a mailman. . . .

NAZIM HIKMET
Translated by Randy Blasing and Mutlu Konuk

The Bridge

 Poetry is a river
And solitude a bridge.

Through writing
    We cross it,
Through reading

We return.

KAISSAR AFIF
Translated by Mansour Ajami

Give Birth to Me Again That I May Know

Give birth to me again . . . Give birth to me again that I may know
      in which land I will die, in which land I will come to life again.
Greetings to you as you light the morning fire, greetings to you,
      greetings to you.
Isn't it time for me to give you some presents, to return to you?
Is your hair still longer than our years, longer than the trees of clouds
      stretching the sky to you so they can live?
Give birth to me again so I can drink the country's milk from you and
      remain a little boy in your arms, remain a little boy
For ever. I have seen many things, mother, I have seen. Give birth to
      me again so you can hold me in your hands.
When you feel love for me, do you still sing and cry about nothing?
      Mother! I have lost my hands
On the waist of a woman of a mirage. I embrace sand, I embrace a
      shadow. Can I come back to you/to myself?
Your mother has a mother, the fig tree in the garden has clouds.
      Don't leave me alone, a fugitive. I want your hands
To carry my heart. I long for the bread of your voice, mother!
      I long for everything. I long for myself . . . I long for you.

MAHMOUD DARWISH

Translated by Abdullah al-Udhari

Mother Palestine, Suleiman Mansour

The Home Within

Once upon a tear
I tired of my fear
And my heart whispered
It's time to return

To my lonesome mommy
And my graying daddy
And the hills of olive
And shimmering dandelion.

So I packed my yearning
And began my journey
Until I arrived
At the soldiered border
That divides my world.

I handed my card
And stood in prayer
That I'd be allowed inside
Till a cold voice inquired
Didn't you know?
Time has elapsed
And your permit has expired.
Have you business there?

Sir, I don't have a business;
I have my daddy and my mommy
And many people who know me.
But that's not enough,
The guard declared.

His eyes trailed off slowly;
Then he sealed the window
And turned away.

That night I searched
For a refuge from my hurt
But could see no vein
But the path within.

From there I soared
Beyond frontier and guard
And I quickly arrived
At the old stone house
With the green door.

My father's arms
Rushed to surround me
And his thousand tears
Reached to receive me.
They cried in unison
Welcome home.

IBTISAM S. BARAKAT

The Beginning of the Road

He read each day like a book
and saw the world as a lantern
in the night of his fury.
He saw the horizon come to him
as a friend.
He read directions
in the faces of poetry and fire.

ADONIS
Translated by Samuel Hazo

Freedom

Alone, now you are free
You pick a sky and name it
    a sky to live in
    a sky to refuse
But to know that you are free
and to remain free
you must steady yourself on a foothold of earth
so that the earth may rise
so that you may give wings to all
the children of the earth

SAADI YOUSSEF
Translated by Khaled Mattawa

Enough for Me

Enough for me to die on her earth
be buried in her
to melt and vanish into her soil
then sprout forth as a flower
played with by a child from my country
Enough for me to remain
in my country's embrace
to be in her close as a handful of dust
    a sprig of grass
        a flower.

FADWA TUQAN
*Translated by Salma Khadra Jayyusi and
Naomi Shihab Nye*

from *Stone for a Sling*

...i played
games with child friends whose names i forgot
i was the best at grabbing the five stones off the ground
thanks to those five stones in one hand
i could never ever hold a sling to kill birds...

then i saw life-size cartoons of wars, of massacres, of genocide...
of fingerprints crying out for their owners...
of human beings indifferent to human affliction...

now in my room with birds from all over the world
i play hide-and-seek in poems
hoping to shed light onto lullabies...
hoping not to be
the stone for a sling.

YUSUF ERADAM

Golrokh and Her Grandmother, Kobra Ebrahimi

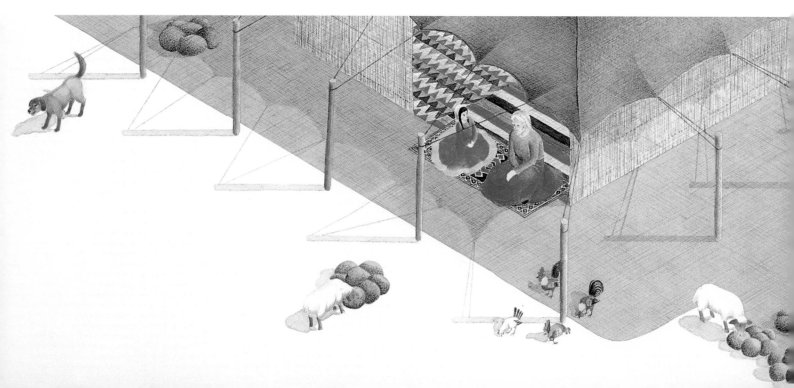

Home

The world map
colored yellow and green
draws a straight line from Massachusetts to Egypt.

Homesick for the streets
filthy with the litter
of people, overfilled so you must
look to put your next step down;
bare feet and *galabiyas** pinch
you into a spot tighter
than a net full of fish,

drivers bound out
of their hit cars
to battle in the streets
and cause a jam as mysterious
as the building of the pyramids,

sidewalk cafes with overgrown men
heavy suited, play backgammon
and bet salaries from absent jobs,

gypsies lead their carts
with chanting voices,
tempting with the smell of crisp fried *falafel***
and cumin spiced fava beans,

sweetshops
display their *baklava* and *basboosa*†
glistening with syrup
browned like the people who make them,

women, hair and hands henna red
their eyes, *khol*-lined†† and daring.

The storms gather from the ground
dust and dirt mixed into the sand,
a whirlwind flung into my eyes,

I fly across
and land—
hands pressing into rooted earth.

PAULINE KALDAS

galabiyas—kaftan-like clothes worn by Egyptians
**falafel*—delicious fried chick pea patties
†*baklava* and *basboosa*—popular Arabic sweets
††*khol*—eyeliner (make-up)

Untitled, Rabab Nemr

I Have No Address

I am a sparrow with a white heart and a thousand tongues.
I fly around the globe
Singing for peace, love and humanity
In every place.
I have no address.

My address is lines ornamented by dreams, beating hearts united by smiling hope
For people who wish good for other people all the time.
I sing, smile and cry.
My tears wash away pain
In every place.

Our paths are boats of longing, turning round and round with us—
One day to the east, another to the west, to tranquil moorings.
And when the waves go against us and cast us away,
Then the echo of my sounds at midnight will be a dock at the shore of tranquility,
In every place.

The day we join hands with others' hands, our universe is
A rose garden blooming in the holy night.
It contains us, with hope, love and alleluias.

And I am the sparrow on the branch.
I sleep, dream and fly happily
In every place.
I have no address.

HAMZA EL DIN

from Memoirs in Exile

I roam from one end of time to the other,
holding in hand
my pen, my palette and my chisel.
As I look about me
I feel crippled, I've forgotten what it is
to run or jump.
I lean on my body like a cane
to cross the little space of earth
people call a homeland.

A white dot bores through a black page.
A child's tear
soaks through all the slogans.

The battle quieted down.
The old woman poked her head in
and shouted,
—Don't leave anything behind.
Ignorant people might pick your remnants up
and write our children's history with them.

Tomorrow looms in sight.
The homeland will return.
We will throw our wanderings and our suitcases
into the sea.

JOSEPH ABI DAHER
Translated by Adnan Haydar and Michael Beard

The Land Across the Valley

quotes from Rashid Hussein

You always told me to remember stories
about our village, and to remember
the songs that carry the legends of our land;
and to remember the faces of old women,
for in them is our history.
Isn't that so?

My father heard my words and turned away
to look across the valley to where our land is.
Teach the night to forget to bring
dreams showing me my village,
he said and then was quiet again.
His silence fell on us as the sun burned

the stones we sat on. I tried to taste
the breeze coming up from the valley.
And teach the wind to forget to carry to me
the aroma of apricots in my fields.
We looked to the other side of the valley,
at the olive trees and red poppies

scattering the hillsides.
"There is no god but Allah,"
sang a distant muezzin.
And teach the sky, too, to forget to rain.
My father closed his eyes.
Only then, may I forget my country.

LAILA HALABY

To Everything There Is a Season, Ghada Jamal

"There was in our house a river"

Poem

Without paper or pen
        into your heart I reach
Listening is more poignant
        than any speech.

FAWZIYYA ABU KHALID
Translated by Salwa Jabsheh and John Heath-Stubbs

Talk

You never hear it
but at breakfast the sweetest talk
is between the jam and the honey.

GÖKHAN TOK
Translated by Yusuf Eradam

Untitled

The woman is waiting
She sits on the seashore
The moon rests between her palms
And her face illuminates the silver wave.

♦ ♦ ♦

When the sun rises
I pull the curtains
Light streams into my room
And the street sinks in darkness.

♦ ♦ ♦

A cloud of ash on the cup's brim
As I sit alone in the café
Drinking the morning melancholy.

ABDULLAH HABIB ALMAAINI
Translated by the author

Waitress

One of the waitresses
            at Berlin's Astoria Restaurant
        was a jewel of a girl.
She'd smile at me across her heavy trays.
She looked like the girls of the country I've lost.
Sometimes she had dark circles under her eyes—
             I don't know why.
I never got to sit
      at one of her tables.

He never once sat at one of my tables.
He was an old man.
And he must have been sick—
            he was on a special diet.
He could gaze at my face so sadly,
            but he couldn't speak German.
For three months he came in for three meals a day,
then he disappeared.
Maybe he went back to his country,
            maybe he died before he could.

NAZIM HIKMET

Translated by Randy Blasing and Mutlu Konuk

Letters to My Mother

Good morning, sad priestess
& a kiss for your wet cheek.
It's me! Sinbad
your senseless son who
many moons ago
took off on his fantastic voyage.
Don't you remember how he packed
the green morning of home
inside his faded bag! What finesse
stuffing his clean underwear
with little bundles of dried mint leaves.

I'm alone now.
The smoke bores the cigarette.
The typewriter is bored.
My pains are birds
searching for a nest.
Yes, I've known women in America:
cement sentiments
& beauty carved of wood.

Greetings to our large house
to my bed & books
to the children of our block
to walls we decorated with chaotic writing
to lazy cats sleeping on windowsills
covered with lilacs.

Twelve years now, Mother
since I left Tangier.
November is here

He brings his presents pressingly:
tears & moans at my windowpane
& November is here.
Where is Tangier?
Its saffron suns & listless seas?
Where is Father?
Where are his eyes
& the silk of their look?
Where is the open yard
of our large house?
Carnations chuckled
in the shade of its corners.
Where is my childhood?
I dragged cats by their tails
across the open yard.

I'm alone now.
My pains are birds searching for a nest.

BEN BENNANI

98

The Search for My Grandmother

In this courtyard
feathers and fingers of gold
the cane
her hair   her wooden wedding comb
and that pitcher silent and blue
A kingdom of dust
I shake it off
and it returns like drizzle
I see her
She breathes
staggers forward
staggers back
and explodes with tears
I whisper: Grandmother
I scream: Grandmother
I repeat   I rave
and suddenly
she vanishes in smoke

HATIF JANABI

Translated by Khaled Mattawa

Cat Poem

He came on like a bodiless lion.
"Something is wrong with my friend's condition," I said.

He stated a position, to study all my ambitions.
"My friend's mind has turned upside down," I said.

He leapt and crashed, pretending to be half mad.
"Let my friend eat pebbles," I said.

He howled and blustered from the top of the tree.
"My friend is fall . . . fall . . . falliiiinnng."

He said, "Mee meow." To which I replied, "Hey Hey-ow!"
My friend is an offspring of the kitty-cat kind.

Hop hop hoppety hop hop
My friend hoppety hoppety hop hop

MOHAMMED ASFOUR
Translated by Assef al-Jundi

I Do Not Blame You

Your wings are small for this storm—
I do not blame you.
You're good, and frightened, and
I am the hurricane. I used to be a wing
struggling in the storm
but then I became the storm,
lacking light, shade, or a wise language.
And now I confess
to be a lost planet circling a lost world
and I do not blame you:
What has tender mint to do with the storm?

SAMIH AL-QASIM
Translated by Sharif S. Elmusa and Naomi Shihab Nye

"10"

Five butterflies lived in a house near the river.
Every morning they energetically went out to collect
music of the flowers.
One day one of them returned carrying a sword of flames.
It declared mutiny.
Soon the walls of the house fell,
the ceiling burned, and in the house
the poems died!

ALI AL-JUNDI
Translated by Assef al-Jundi

Baghdad, Widad al-Orfali

The River

Once
there was in our house a river
magnanimous
delicate steps
My father made his rosary from its minnows
and the carpet we spread was made from its mist
Once
a thief came to our house
He came from beyond the villages
and axes were landed on his neck
and split him in halves
Since then
My father's heart dried up and he died
My sisters ended up in poverty and widowhood
But my mother insisted
on digging the earth
scratching with her fingers
believing water will appear

HASHIM SHAFIQ
Translated by Khaled Mattawa

You Are My Yemen

You are my Yemen and my Damascus
You are the goal of my winter journey and my summer
You are my city and its streets
You are my village and its fields

I shimmy up palm trees to wait for you
To squint into the sun and watch for you
You are my caravan loaded with lentils and cracked wheat
Snaking its way into town
We the city-dwellers trill with joy
Layla and Majnun will fry chopped onions tonight!

You are my neighborhood and my quarter
My children running through the gate, scattering chickens
My women leaning out of windows shrilling,
"Did you get the bundle I left for you at Um Ahmad's?"
My men bringing crates of ripe vegetables
Buthayna and Jamil will cook eggplants in their rice tonight

You are Joha* who appears everywhere
And leaves everyone laughing and gasping
You are the con-artist who takes everything
And leaves the smile on the face
Go ahead, trick me out of my self

You are my Yemen and my Damascus
You are my Cairo and my Baghdad
Your arms are Umayyad minarets
Your thighs are Tigris and Euphrates
Your eyelids are Egyptian cinema screens

You know the lines to all the Shadia** movies
You know the rhymes of all the hanging odes†
Your body moves like the sand dunes of Rub'al-Khali and I am lost in it
You know the flavor of the clumps of rice
that cling to the soft seedy insides of fried eggplant

I fly to you, I roam over
my Yemen, my Damascus
in winter, in summer
my village, my city
my minarets, my rivers

I burst through the gates toward you,
my field, my neighbor
The harvest crates, the trays of rice are gathered
Here is the time of fasting, time of feasting
Here is the call to prayer, trill of joy

Here are the long-awaited evenings!
Here you are. Here am I.
Your face
the horizon
I want to see

MOHJA KAHF

*Joha—the wise fool who appears as folk hero in countless Middle Eastern stories
**Shadia—Egyptian movie star
†hanging odes—the ten (or seven) best poems of pre-Islamic Arabia. For their excellence they were reputedly written (some claim in gold) and
hung upon the ka'ba—the black cubic building that was and is a center of Arab pilgrimage.

Untitled #2, Balqees Fakhro

A Song

When we remember things
One string rings out.
Woman alone
Plays on all the strings
With one stroke
Because she is the entire homeland.

MUHAMMAD AL-AS'AD
Translated by May Jayyusi and Jack Collom

All of Them

Everybody said it was useless
Everybody said, "you're trying to lean on sun dust"
     that the beloved before whose tree I stand
          can't be reached

   Everybody said, "you're crazy to throw yourself
          headlong into a volcano and sing"
   Everybody said that salty mountains
        won't yield even one glass of wine
   Everybody said, "You can't dance on one foot"
   Everybody said there won't be any lights at the party
   That's what they all said
   but everybody came to the party anyway

QASIM HADDAD
Translated by Sharif S. Elmusa and Charles Doria

Electrons

Atoms within your body
spin.
What seems solid—
knees, nose, hair—
moves swiftly. Particles
orbit each other. Dart like meteors
through vast spaces.

Air about you
made of same.
You take from it
and you give.
Drawing in atoms and molecules
to form
your ever changing image.

Your lips move.
Your tongue speaks your name.
You take it on faith your words will make sense.
Meaning flows out effortlessly.

Electrons
skip like rocks on water
between your solid body
and your electromagnetic thoughts.
You look through a window.
Listen to voices from within and without.

Dazzled by what you perceive,
you wonder about causes and effects.

When a wave of love takes you by surprise,
your eyes well up with tears.

ASSEF AL-JUNDI

108

New Year's Eve, Riham Ghassib

Hebron, Nabil Anani

from *Thread by Thread*

Thread by thread
knot by knot
like colonies of ants
we weave a bridge

Thread by thread
piece by piece
knitting embroidering
sewing decorating
thread by thread
we weave
the map of conciliation.

Rachel's is white
Yemima's purple
Amal's is green
Salima's rose-colored
thread by thread
we stitch together
torn hearts
bind the map of conciliation.

I pray for the life of Ami and Nitsi
you pray for Ilan, Shoshi and Itsik
and she prays
for Jehan, Asheraf and Fahed
with the same tear.
Word and another word
prayer and another prayer
and our heart is one
we embroider in hope

with the sisterhood of workers
a map of love
to tear down the borders. . .

BRACHA SERRI
Translated by Shlomit Yaacobi and Nava Mizrahhi

Grandfather

Your grandchildren
are climbing
the oak tree in the backyard
on the planks of wood
you nailed in its side
Soon they will not remember
who spaced them so evenly
Do you feel the weight
of a small foot on your heart,
and when they reach the top
will you grasp their hands
and hoist them up with you?

MOHJA KAHF

The Deserted Well

I knew Ibrahim
my dear neighbor
from way back. I knew
him overflowing with water
like a well people passed by
without stopping to drink
or even, even to drop
a stone.

When the enemy aimed
their cannon of death
and the soldiers rushed
under a hail of death
and shelling, *retreat! retreat!*
it was shouted, *in the shelter
back there, you shall
be safe from death
and shelling.*
But Ibrahim
kept marching on
his tiny breast filling
the horizon, he marched forward
*retreat! retreat!
in the shelter back there
you shall be safe
from death
and shelling.*
But Ibrahim
as though he didn't hear

kept on marching.
They said it was madness.
Maybe it was madness.
But I had known
my dear neighbor Ibrahim
from way back. From childhood I knew him
overflowing with water
like a well people passed by
without stopping to drink
or even, even to drop
a stone

YUSUF AL-KHAL
Translated by Sargon Boulus

112

everyone knows
that little loves will end
suddenly for no clear reason
one day they'll end
silently like the coming of night or death

everyone knows from the start
that little lives will end
and afterwards everything will be forgotten
like war news
summer rains
and reproachful letters

is there one who remembers a meal in the country
the pink of the mallow-flower
swarms of ants
is there one who remembers
the color of anyone's eyes
or the name
of the poet whose heart
was always open
like the gate of an inn

MELISA GÜRPINAR
Translated by Ruth Christie

A Day in the Life of Nablus

We fall, not on our knees, but on our hearts

——Vassar Miller

-1-
Summer. The figs are bruise pink,
tomatoes luscious enough
to stop a hurried man.
Ignore the flies.
At 9 a.m. peasants savor *shish-kebab*
in puny, vaulted eateries.
Ah, the roasting coffee's aroma,
the folklore of each of the senses

This is a place for commerce.
Everything here is for sale:
children's toys, kitchen utensils,
bananas, peanuts, pinenuts, posters,
cassettes, straw mats, sponge mats, watches,
Elvis' T-shirts, turkey breasts, shoes.

The vendor in dishevelled clothes
arranges a feast of pears,
lifts one with pride
as he might his own child.
He bellows into the air:
Go to sleep with a sweet mouth.
He sees the soldiers.
He does not brood over power or history.

-2-
No curfew
during our five-week stay.

-3-
Walking on University Boulevard,
I spot soldiers manning a checkpoint:
the school has been ordered shut.
And, as if in the recurring dream,
I frisk myself for my passport
but find my pockets empty.
I go past the black machine guns
thinking how as a boy
I caught black wasps
and removed their stingers.

A few yards away from the checkpoint
I read a sign:
Office of Reconciliation.
Inside, a Samaritan rabbi
clad in brown caftan and red turban
is ensconced on a couch, waiting,
resigned to waiting.

-4-
On an immaculate wall
of a friend's living room
hangs a picture in a gilded frame:
a woman squatting amidst the rubble
of her house demolished by the army,
cheek cupped in hand,
peering into a white, empty bucket.

-5-

In cafes men congregate in the afternoons,
slowly sip their tea
(as if time were their own),
shuffle cards, spur the backgammon dice
(as if chance were their own).
They listen to songs
of unrequited love, promises unkept, partings.
When the sun sinks behind the hills
they salute the fading day, irreconciled,
leaving the folded market
to the screech of armored cars.

6-

The sky flowers tonight.
The Stars are bright and real
as children's eyes
as the faces of women loved
after years of waiting.
A meteor dives like a deft acrobat.
A satellite sails west to east, unperturbed.
Is it Russian or American?
A scientist or a spy?
Or a station where voices
of distant lovers dovetail?

In gowns of soft lights
the town performs the ritual of sleep.
Will the vendor,
will the woman who lost her house
sleep with a sweet mouth?
The settlement, fortress on the mountain
     peak,
and the jail on the hilltop
flood their dreams with yellow lights.

I want the kind breeze
the power of pears
the sound of the flute,
melodious and sad
like the hills of this land,
to grant us all,
vendors and soldiers,
grant us ample love
that we may turn this troubled page
that we may sleep with a sweet mouth.

Sharif S. Elmusa

115

Untitled, Adar Or-Yosef

Point of Departure

Hidden in the study at dusk,
I wait, not yet lonely.
A heavy walnut bureau opens up the night.
The clock is a tired sentry,
its steps growing faint.

From where? In Grandfather's typewriter,
an Underwood from ancient times,
thousands of alphabets are ready.
What tidings?

I think that not everything is in doubt.
I follow the moment, not to let it slip away.
My arms are rather thin.
I am nine years old.

Beyond the door begins
the interstellar space which I'm ready for.
Gravity drains from me like colors at dusk.
I fly so fast that I'm motionless
and leave behind me
the transparent wake of the past.

DAN PAGIS
Translated by Stephen Mitchell

Quintrain

Once . . . I heard a bird,
an absorbed, ecstatic bird,
eloquently telling
its child:
"Fly away,
soar high:
a few bread crumbs
will suffice you,
but the sky
you need . . .
the whole sky."

Sa'id 'Aql

Translated by Mansour Ajami

THE

MIDDLE

EAST

MOROCCO

ALGERIA

TUNISIA

LIBYA

N

W

E

S

NOTES ON THE CONTRIBUTORS

ADONIS (b. 1930, Syria) is one of the most widely loved poets, critics, translators, philosophers, and presenters of poetry in the Arab world. He works in literary journalism in Lebanon and has published many books, including *The Pages of Day and Night*.

MAMDOUH ADWAN (b. 1941, Syria) lived in Quayroun village as a child, and graduated from Damascus University. He has worked as a journalist and published numerous collections of poetry and dramas. He had a Smithsonian fellowship to the United States in 1994.

KAISSAR AFIF was born and grew up in Lebanon. He studied philosophy, focusing on Heidigger and Zen. He founded an international journal of modern Arabic poetry called *al-Haraka al-Shi'riyya*. Poet, critic, translator, and educator, he currently resides in Mexico.

MANSOUR AJAMI was born and raised in Lebanon, and currently resides in Princeton, New Jersey. He received his B.A. and M.A. in Arabic literature and philosophy from the American University of Beirut and writes poetry in both Arabic and English. The poem printed here was written for his son Nassim when he was seven.

GÜLTEN AKIN (b. 1933) is one of Turkey's most distinguished and quoted women poets, for whom "poetry is synonymous with social responsibility." She has worked widely as a lawyer in Anatolia. Author of many collections and recipient of many awards, she currently lives in Ankara.

LAYLA 'ALLUSH (b. 1948, Palestine) has written extensively about life under occupation. Her first book was called *Spices on the Open Wound*.

ABDULLAH HABIB ALMAAINI (b. 1964, Oman) earned a *cum laude* B.A. in philosophy and is currently doing graduate work in film studies. He has published poetry and fiction, as well as articles and translations, was awarded the Silver Prize of the UAE Cultural Foundation for one of his short films, and co-founded the Omani Film Association in 1996. The author writes: "I believe in the silent whiteness of the page which crouches around words, securing, interpreting, and expanding them."

SAWSAN AMER (Egypt) is the director of the Art Research Unit at the Academy of the Arts in Egypt, and a professor on the faculty of art education. She has written a book and many articles on folk art, and her work is widely exhibited.

YEHUDA AMICHAI is Israel's most popular poet and lives in Jerusalem with his wife, Hana Sokolov Amichai. His work has been translated into thirty-three languages. He has published poetry, novels, and a collection of short stories, *The World is a Room*. When the Nobel Peace Prize was awarded to Yitzhak Rabin, Shimon Peres, and Yasir Arafat together in Oslo, Amichai read "Wildpeace," which appears in *This Same Sky* (Simon & Schuster).

NABIL ANANI (b. 1943, Palestine) is a painter, ceramicist, and art teacher. He uses a variety of symbols and cultural motifs in his art, reflecting a deep sense of anxiety and love for his homeland. He is a member of the league of Palestinian Artists in the Occupied Territories and participates in their exhibitions in the Middle East and elsewhere.

SA'ID 'AQL (b. 1912, Lebanon) is well-known for influencing Arabic poetry toward Symbolism. One of his books is called *More Beautiful Than You, No!*

ÖZDEMIR ASAF (1923-1981) lived in Ankara and was known to be the "poet of the art of paradox." He gave up studying law and economy for journalism and printing. He is one of the most popular, frequently-quoted poets in current Turkey.

MOHAMMED ASFOUR teaches in the Department of English at the Al-Ain University in the United Arab Emirates.

HANAN MIKHA'IL 'ASHRAWI (b. 1946, Palestine) became known worldwide for her efforts in the cause of Palestinian-Israeli negotiations toward peace. Her recent autobiographical book is *This Side of Peace* (Simon & Schuster). She attended Friends Girls School as a child in Ramallah, later getting her doctorate in medieval English Literature and heading the English Department at Bir Zeit University. She lives in Ramallah with her husband, a musician, and two daughters.

MUHAMMAD AL-AS'AD (b. 1944, Palestine) grew up first in a village near Haifa, but his family eventually moved to Iraq after becoming refugees in 1948. He has worked as a journalist in Kuwait, has published an autobiography, poetry, and criticism, and currently lives in Cyprus.

FOUZI EL-ASMAR (b. 1937, Haifa) received his Ph.D. from the University of Exeter, England, in Islamic and Arabic Studies. He has published many books, including *Dreams on a Mattress of Thorns*, and lectures and teaches widely. He has also been a news agency bureau chief.

SUAD AL-ATTAR (b. 1942, Iraq) was the first Iraqi woman artist to have a solo exhibition in Baghdad. She has studied in Iraq, California, and London, and her work is exhibited in museums worldwide. Her work reflects a dreamy world of symbols rooted in the history of ancient Mesopotamian civilizations.

THURAYA AL-BAQSAMI (b. 1952, Kuwait) began painting before she was ten, and became a member of the Kuwait Formative Art Society at the age of seventeen. She has exhibited her work in Kuwait, Senegal, Switzerland, England, and Greece, and also organized a project creating wall drawings in children's wards of Kuwaiti hospitals. A strong advocate of women's rights, she is a frequent contributor to Kuwaiti magazines and newspapers and runs an art gallery with her husband.

IBTISAM S. BARAKAT grew up in the occupied territories of Palestine and attended Birzeit University where she studied English literature. She came to the United States to study journalism and human development, has written for children and been a publications editor, and currently lives in Missouri.

SALEEM BARAKAT (b. 1951, Syria) is of Kurdish origin. He has lived in Beirut and Cyprus and has edited *Al-Karmel*, the literary review for the Palestinian Union of Writers. He is known for writing about animals, which used to be popular in classical Arabic poetry, but is rarely done today.

ABDUL WAHAB AL-BAYATI (b. 1926, Iraq) studied at Baghdad Teachers College and worked as a teacher, then a journalist. He has lived in Lebanon, Syria, Egypt, Austria, and Moscow, and is considered one of the most important representatives of the "socialist realist school" in modern Arabic poetry.

ZEYNEP BELER (b. 1985, Ankara) started painting when she was a baby. She attended school in Turkey till the fifth grade, then in California, and is now back in Turkey. She likes reading and writing poems and stories, and has had three exhibitions of her paintings.

BEN BENNANI (b. 1946, Lebanon) was educated in classical Arabic literature in Tripoli. He has taught writing, translation, and literature in the United States and in Bahrain. His poems and translations have been published widely; one of his collections of poems is called *Camel's Bite*.

EREZ BITON (b. 1942, Algeria) currently lives in Tel Aviv. Blinded as a child by a grenade he picked up in an orchard, he was educated at an institution for the blind. He worked as a social worker and psychologist in the Social Welfare Services, but has recently devoted himself to writing poetry, including *Moroccan Offering, The Book of Mint*, and *A Bird Between Continents*. Long devoted to bringing writers, artists, and intellectuals together, he gives performances of his poetry with musical accompaniment.

SALIH BOLAT (b. 1956, Adana) studied sociology and politics in Ankara, Turkey, has published four poetry collections, and won various awards. He works at Hacettepe University.

DAOUD BOULOS (b. 1950, Kafr Yasif, the Galilee) studied in his village, later coming to the United States for higher studies in TV and motion picture directing. He is currently involved in writing and directing children's TV programs for Arabs and Jews and a major motion picture based on a script he wrote: "Don Quixote Comes from the West Bank." He lives with his family in the half-Arab, half-Jewish village of Neve Shalom/Wahat al-Salam ("village of peace") high on a hilltop north of Jerusalem.

KAMEL BRAHIM (b. 1950, Tunisia) grew up in Tunisia and moved to Paris at the age of thirty. He studied at the Ecole des Beaux Arts in Tunis, and has had many individual and group exhibitions of his artwork.

OMAR BSOUL (b. 1951, Jordan) is a self-taught artist. He works with unusual materials, such as wax, crayons, and pastels, creating a remarkable texture. His art incorporates elements from northern Jordanian folklore as well as Islamic calligraphy.

EDIP CANSEVER (1928–1986) grew up in Istanbul. He started publishing his many books in 1944 and received numerous awards for his work.

ALI CENGIZKAN (b. 1954, Ankara) graduated from Middle East Technical University, Department of Architecture, where he is now the chairman. He published his first book of poetry in 1977 and has won many awards.

SHLOMIT COHEN-ASSIF is a native Israeli who lives and writes in Holon. A prolific author of children's books, poems, and fairy tales, she reads her work widely and received the 1996 ACUM prize for Life Contribution to the Arts.

JOSEPH ABI DAHER (b. 1947, Lebanon) entered the world of journalism early. He has founded literary magazines, published books of poetry, written hundreds of TV and radio shows, and songs and plays for children. He is also a painter. UNICEF awarded him a prize for his children's songs in 1986.

MAHMOUD DARWISH (b. 1942, Palestine) is one of the most well-known voices worldwide for the Palestinian people. He grew up in Birwa and Haifa and has also lived in Egypt, Lebanon, and Paris. Recently he was honored by the French government for his work. His eloquent poems have been described as being "right in there with the best of this century" by American poet James Tate.

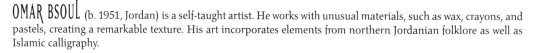

REZA DE RAKSHANI (Iran) is both a painter and a musician, and his visual art embraces both modern techniques and the traditional imagery of Persian art. "De Rakshani's lushly colored, richly textured canvases combine a Persian intricacy and ornateness with aggressive Western gesturalism to acheive a uniquely opulent beauty," an art critic praised. De Rakshani's work has been exhibited widely in Iran, the United States, and Europe.

HAMZA EL DIN (b. 1929, Wadi-Halfa, near the Egypt-Sudan border) has been called "the living ambassador of Nubian music." He began playing the *oud* and vocalizing during college. The village he lived in as a child was flooded by the construction of the Aswan Dam. He describes his introduction to Arabic popular music: "At that time in Egypt, between every coffee shop and the next coffee shop, there was a coffee shop, and each coffee shop had a radio. When you walked down the street you continuously heard music." He travels widely to perform.

ZUHUR DIXON (b. 1933, Iraq) has lived in Baghdad for many years, though she grew up south of Basra. Her poetry conveys "a deep message of freedom and individuality." One of her books is called *A Homeland for Everything.*

MOSHE DOR was born in Tel Aviv and has published numerous volumes of poetry and literary essays. He worked as a journalist for many years. He has been Counsellor for Cultural Affairs at the Israeli Embassy in England, Distinguished Writer-in-Residence at the American University in Washington, D.C., and was elected president of the Israeli PEN organization. He has received many honors, including the Prime Minister's Prize and the Bialik Prize, Israel's top literary award.

KOBRA EBRAHIMI (b. 1962, Iran) has exhibited her works both in Iran and abroad, and has won awards from UNICEF among others. She lives in Teheran and illustrates children's books.

INJI EFFLATOUN (1924-1989, Egypt) studied design and painting in France, and participated in the exhibitions of the Art and Freedom Group. Her artwork was inspired by Egypt's villagers and peasants. A strong supporter of women's rights, she was jailed for her political activism in 1960 and continued to paint in prison. Her works are exhibited in museums and private collections around the world.

ORA EITAN was born in Tel Aviv, and studied art at the Bezalel Academy in Jerusalem. She is a fine artist and an illustrator of children's books, including *Sun Is Falling, Night Is Calling* (Simon & Schuster), which has been compared to the children's classic *Goodnight Moon*. She lives in Jerusalem.

SALWA ARNOUS ELAYDI (b. 1946, Palestine) has lived in Palestine, Lebanon, Egypt, Kuwait, and the United States. She sees her art as a means of expressing and informing others about the sufferings of the Palestinian people. Artists who have influenced her work include Georgia O'Keeffe, Henri Matisse, and René Magritte.

SHELLEY ELKAYAM (b. 1955, Haifa) lives in Jerusalem and is described as being "a tireless activist in peace, women's, educational, and social issues." She has written children's books, published poems, and been a delegate to many international conferences.

SHARIF S. ELMUSA (b. 1947, Palestine) was the fifth child in a family made refugees within a year of his birth. His father grew figs, grapes, and oranges outside Jaffa till the family moved to the Nuweimeh refugee camp in Jericho. Twelve children were raised in all. Elmusa attended Cairo University and later received his Ph.D. from M.I.T. He is an expert on agrarian development and water issues, has returned to the Middle East with his family on a Fulbright scholarship, and currently lives in Washington, D.C.

YUSUF ERADAM (b. 1954, Turkey) is a prolific poet, translator, short story writer, songwriter, and editor currently teaching American Literature at Ankara University.

SALAH FA'IQ (b. 1945, Iraq) left school at the age of fifteen and has worked as a journalist and literary editor. He has published collections of prose poetry.

GÜRBÜZ DOĞAN EKŞİOĞLU (b. 1954, Turkey) is one of Turkey's leading illustrators, and has won awards both in Turkey and internationally. His work has appeared on the covers of *The New Yorker* and *Forbes* as well as many other magazines and newspapers.

BALQEES FAKHRO (b. 1950, Bahrain) studied art in San Francisco and is an active member of the Bahrain Society of Formative Art. She is an art critic and lecturer as well as an artist.

FATIMA HASSAN EL-FAROUJ (b. 1945, Morocco), a self-taught artist, has exhibited her artwork widely in the Arab world as well as in Europe. Her work records the daily life of women in Morocco, depicting the traditions and rituals associated with marriage, childbirth, and religion.

RIHAM GHASSIB (Jordan) grew up in Jordan and studied at Kansas State University. Her artwork, which reflects Jordanian country and urban life, has been exhibited both in Jordan and the United States, and has been the subject of a television special.

MUHAMMAD AL-GHUZZI (b. 1949, Tunisia) attended the Tunisian University and has worked as a teacher in his ancient hometown of Qairwan, a traditional center of Islamic learning. He has also translated Swedish poetry into Arabic.

MELISA GÜRPINAR (b. 1941) is a poet and playwright living in Istanbul. She graduated from the Istanbul Conservatory and also studied drama in London and prepared programs for the BBC. She has published many books of poems.

QASIM HADDAD (b. 1948, Bahrain) left secondary school before graduation and later became Director of Culture and Art at the Ministry of Information. He has also headed the Union of Bahraini Writers and published numerous collections.

LAILA HALABY was born in Lebanon, the daughter of a Jordanian father and American mother. She currently lives in Los Angeles and is fluent in Spanish, Arabic, Italian, and French. She has Master's degrees in Arabic Literature and counseling and recently had a Fulbright scholarship to Jordan.

SUHEIR HAMMAD (b. 1973, Jordan) is the daughter of Palestinian refugee parents. Her family lived in Beirut during part of the Civil

War, then immigrated to Brooklyn, New York. She is devoted to "giving voice to those who have been silenced for so long." Her books are *Drops of This Story* and *Born Palestinian, Born Black.*

NATHALIE HANDAL was born in 1969. Her parents are both from Bethlehem, Palestine. She grew up in many places including the Caribbean and Europe, but returns to the Middle East often. She received her M.A. in Literature in Boston and is now an independent researcher/scholar writing and lecturing on Arabic women writers and Arab-American writers. She loves music, reading, traveling, writing poetry, and learning, learning, learning...

SALMAN HARRATI writes poetry in Iran.

FAIK HASSAN (b. 1914, Iraq) is known as the pioneer of modern Arab art in the Islamic world. His intense and somber paintings bring to light the poverty and suffering of the Iraqi people, but also celebrate their strength and endurance.

NAZIM HIKMET (1902-1963) is considered the poet laureate of Turkey. He was a political prisoner in Turkey for nineteen years and spent the last thirteen years of his life in exile. His work was banned in Turkey for decades. Many of his filmscripts, plays, essays, and novels were published after his death. Now he is revered and quoted worldwide by people supporting human rights and peace.

MOHAMMED AFIF HUSSAINI is a Syrian poet living in Sweden.

GHADA JAMAL (b. 1954, Lebanon) divides her time between California, England, and Lebanon. "In my early years in Lebanon I painted on location, depicting the poetic serenity of the Lebanese landscapes." In the mid-80s, she left war-torn Lebanon to pursue painting in the United States. "I reacted to the situation and what I had left behind; my anger and dismay found violent expression in large canvases laden with thick potent colors." Today, her paintings represent dreamlike images of an earlier time, "the soft lament of a lost dream."

HATIF JANABI is a native of Iraq who has lived in exile in Lebanon and Europe. Recently he has been a visiting professor in the department of Near Eastern Studies at Indiana University.

TAHAR BEN JELLOUN is a novelist and poet of Morocco. He writes in French.

ALI AL-JUNDI lives in Latakia, Syria, on the Mediterranean Sea. He was among the generation of writers that witnessed the birth of a new Syria in 1947 and had great hopes for Arab unity. He has published many poetry collections including *The Broken Banner, In the Beginning There Was Silence, Earthly Fever,* and *Timed Poems.*

ASSEF AL-JUNDI (b. 1952, Damascus) grew up in Syria and came to the United States to study electrical engineering at the University of Texas. He returned to Syria to work in the oil fields where he discovered parts of the country (the desert and the plains along the Turkish and Iraqi borders) that he had not known as a boy. He now lives with his wife Sara in San Antonio, Texas, where he works for a telecommunications company and enjoys camping, golf, and backpacking.

SHAFEE'E KADKANI of Iran is a poet and a university professor in Teheran. His works have been widely known both before and after the revolution.

YEHUDIT KAFRI (b. 1935, Kibbutz Ein Ha Horesh) works in editing, translating, and writing in Israel and has received many awards for her poetry, children's books, memoirs, and biographies.

MOHJA KAHF (b. 1967, Damascus) has also lived in Iraq, Saudi Arabia, and the United Arab Emirates. She received a Ph.D. in Comparative Literature from Rutgers University and currently teaches English and Middle Eastern Studies in Arkansas.

PAULINE KALDAS was born in Egypt and came to the United States in 1969. After several months, she was able to decipher the English language and went on to repeat the fourth grade successfully. She often missed her grandmother, her dog Rita, and the guava tree in her Egyptian backyard. She returned to Egypt more than once and taught at the American University in Cairo. Currently she is working on her Ph.D. in English at Binghamton University.

SHAFIQ AL-KAMALI (1930-1984) lived in Iraq but also studied literature in Egypt. A participant in the ongoing political struggle in his country, he was imprisoned during his youth, but went on under a different administration to become Minister of Youth and Information and head of the Union of Arab Writers.

HELEN KHAL (b. 1932, United States) is the daughter of Lebanese parents. She studied art in New York and Lebanon, is now a painter, teacher, critic, and the author of *The Woman Artist in Lebanon*.

YUSUF AL-KHAL (1917–1987, Lebanon) was the son of a Protestant minister, studied philosophy and worked in the United States, Libya, and Switzerland. He founded the Shi'r quarterly and publishing house which promoted experimental poetry and translated American poets into Arabic. He also did new translations of the New and Old Testaments.

FAWZIYYA ABU KHALID (b. 1955, Saudi Arabia) grew up in Riyadh, studied sociology in the United States, and has taught at the Girls' College of King Saud University. Her first book of poems was published when she was eighteen.

AHMAD MUHAMMAD AL KHALIFA (b. 1930, Bahrain) was born into the ruling family of his country. He studied Arabic literature and has published numerous books.

DHABIYA KHAMIS (b. 1958, the United Arab Emirates) attended university in the United States, worked on her Ph.D. in London, and currently lives in Egypt. She has published many collections of poetry, including *I Am the Woman, the Earth, All the Ribs*, and short stories, and works in literary journalism.

DEEMA SHEHABI KHORSHEED is a Palestinian who grew up in Kuwait. After graduating from Boston University with a master's degree in journalism, she moved to northern California, where she now resides with her husband, Omar.

SAMI MAHDI (b. 1940, Iraq) studied economics in Baghdad and became editor-in-chief of one of Iraq's leading newspapers, *Al-Jumhuriya*. He has published numerous collections of poetry, including *The Questions*.

NAGUIB MAHFOUZ (b. 1911, Egypt) studied philosophy, then worked as a civil servant till his retirement in 1971. He received the Nobel Prize for Literature in 1988 and numerous other prizes for his thirty-five novels and fourteen collections of short stories. He and his wife live in Cairo. In 1994 he was stabbed in the neck outside his home and has made a slow recovery. His newest book is *Echoes of an Autobiography*, from which the piece here is reprinted.

BAYA MAHIEDDINE (b. 1931, Algeria) was adopted at the age of five by a French couple living in Algeria. A self-taught artist who never learned to read or write, she was exhibiting her work in Paris by the age of sixteen. Her paintings, which use many traditional styles and patterns to depict women and their world, attracted the attention of such artists as Pablo Picasso. André Breton wrote, "Baya's work links us back to the world of pleasure . . . . [She] does not only promise paradise, she gives it."

LISA SUHAIR MAJAJ was born to a Palestinian father and an American mother and grew up in Amman, Jordan. Later she studied in Lebanon before moving to the United States. Her relatives reside in Jerusalem, the West Bank, and Jordan. She currently lives with her Greek-Cypriot husband in Massachusetts where she is completing a dissertation on Arab-American literature for the University of Michigan.

SULEIMAN MANSOUR (b. 1947, Palestine) is a versatile artist, using a variety of styles and media from chalk to wood, straw, and brass. He often uses his artwork to make strong political statements.

KHALED MATTAWA was born and attended primary school in Libya. He immigrated to the United States at the age of 15, later earning both an M.A. in English and an M.F.A. in creative writing from Indiana University. He has been a professor at California State University,

Northridge, and a recipient of the Alfred Hodder Fellowship at Princeton in 1995-1996 and a Guggenheim fellowship for 1997-98. His first collection of poems is *Ismaila Eclipse*.

HASSAN AL-MULLA (b. 1951, Bahrain) studied at the Academy of Fine Arts in Baghdad. Many of his paintings reflect the traditional life of the countryside. He exhibits his work regularly in the Arab world and in Europe, and is currently the director of Qatar's Cultural Center.

MAY MANSOOR MUNN (b. 1934, Jerusalem) loved to read as a child and often rode the bus to the library, where the western novels of Zane Grey gave her an early romanticized impression of the United States. Her father, a physician, and her mother, a teacher, were both Palestinian Quakers. She began writing poetry during the violent times of 1948, when thousands of Palestinians lost homes and property to the new state of Israel. At fifteen she traveled via ocean liner to the United States to attend college, leaving four younger sisters behind. Later she returned home to work as a teacher and disc jockey. She now lives in Texas with her American husband and travels regularly to the Middle East.

AHMAD NAWASH (b. 1934, Jerusalem) studied in Rome and France, and became a leading figure of contemporary Jordanian art. His deeply colored linear compositions combine a rich use of color with an unusual sense of form. They portray the relationship between the individual and society, and offer subtle commentary on political and social issues.

RABAB NEMR (Egypt) studied art in Alexandria and Madrid, and has exhibited widely in Egypt and the Middle East. Her work is displayed in museums in Yugoslavia, Paris, and Jordan. She currently lives in Rome.

AKBAR NIKONPOUR (b. 1956, Iran) studied painting at the University of Teheran. He is an award-winning artist, and his work has been exhibited throughout Europe as well as in Japan and Korea.

WIDAD AL-ORFALI runs an independent art gallery in Baghdad, Iraq.

ADAR OR-YOSEF (Israel) was born in Paris, and studied in Israel and New York. He now lives, paints, and photographs in Israel.

OVISSI (Iran) has exhibited his artwork throughout the world, from Canada to Yugoslavia. His works were featured in the Biennials of Paris, Venice, and São Paulo, and he has been awarded many international prizes, among them the Gold Medal of Italy and the Grand Prix of Monaco.

DAN PAGIS (1930—1986) spent three years in a Nazi concentration camp, moved to Israel at age sixteen, and taught in a kibbutz. He received a doctorate from Hebrew University, where he became a professor. He also taught in the United States, and published many books of poetry, including *Brain*.

MUHAMMAD AL-QAISI (b. 1944, Palestine) grew up in refugee camps after 1948. His poems were influenced by folk songs sung by his mother and neighbor women. He lived in many Arab countries before moving to Jordan in 1977, and has published many poetry collections, including *Houses on the Horizon*.

SAMIH AL-QASIM (b. 1939, Jordan) is a Palestinian living in Nazareth. He has said, "The only way I can assert my identity is by writing poetry." He has worked as a journalist, run a press and a folk arts center, read his poems widely, and been imprisoned many times for his political activities. He has also said, "I feel there is no spiritual difference between Baghdad or Tunis or Jerusalem. I feel that all those countries belong to me. They are my homeland."

ABDUL-RAHEEM SALEH AL-RAHEEM (b. 1950, Iraq) received an M.A. in counseling and has been publishing his poems in Iraqi newspapers and magazines since the 70s. He is married and has six children. "The Train of the Stars" is the title poem of his new book.

DAHLIA RAVIKOVITCH (b. 1936, Ramat Gan) lives in Israel and has published widely known books of poetry, short stories, and children's verse. Her poems are said to convey "a child's sense of wonder and terror."

TOVA REZNICEK (b. 1974, United States) spent most of her childhood on Kibbutz Mishmar Ha'Emek in Israel. She is now studying religion and fine art in New York, and plans to return to Israel one day. She hopes that her art can help to bring greater appreciation and understanding among people. "When this is achieved," she says, "we will truly be able to live side by side without fear or hatred."

FUAD RIFKA (b. 1930, Lebanon) has a Ph.D. in philosophy and lives and teaches in Beirut. He has published many collections of poems.

WAFAA AL-SABBAGH (United Arab Emirates) has had several exhibitions in the Arabian Gulf and has received awards for her graphic art work.

MOHAMAD M. SAMARA (b. 1954, Jordan) sends a strong political message with his artwork, a harsh commentary on the suffering of the poor and dispossessed in Jordan. Much of his work centers around life in the Palestinian refugee camps in Jordan.

SAÂD SARHAN (b. 1961, Morocco) has worked since 1984 as a math teacher in Marrakesh.

GLADYS ALAM SAROYAN writes: "'Unveiled' is about becoming visible. I was born invisible in Beirut, Lebanon. I was not a male, or even a girl of unusual beauty. My hair is black, my eyes are brown . . . I am the middle child of a family of five . . . (Now) I am unveiling. And to my surprise, under my veil, smiles a real face." This is her first publication in a book.

MONA SA'UDI (b. 1945, Jordan) is a sculptor living on the edge of Amman in a house she designed. She writes: "When I was digging the foundation, I found hundreds of small pieces of old pottery, some as old as thousands of years. In this place, I feel eternal life, I smell the human beings who lived on this land before me...They were making the pottery, writing poetry, gazing into nature, tilling the soil, planting the onions and the wheat, shepherding the cows and lambs on the hills. And there are still shepherds around my house, living in caves in the mountains . . . These repetitions of life take me back to our first moment, our beginnings, and a flush of holy love for the earth, light, and stone engulfs me."

LINDA DALAL SAWAYA (United States) grew up in Los Angeles, the daughter of Lebanese parents. She now lives in Portland, Oregon, where she works as a painter, children's book illustrator, photographer, graphic designer, and writer. She works with watercolor, acrylic, oil, and collage using both found and photographic images, and endeavors to make art that is beautiful and humorous, that invokes mystery, brings joy and connection, and that heals.

NAVA SEMEL was born in Tel Aviv, has worked in television, radio, and record production, and is the author of many books, including *Flying Lessons* (Simon & Schuster).

SOHRAB SEPEHRI (b. 1928, Iran) is considered to be one of the most gifted poets writing in Persian. He has published many books and is also a painter.

BRACHA SERRI was born and grew up in Yemen until her family moved to Israel. She has written: "I'm trying to make peace with my pieces. I want my mother's Yemenite culture to be at peace with my father's Jewishness. I want my childhood spoken language, Arabic, to come together with my university education in linguistics . . . I feel I have written my poems for women who do not have a voice, who can't speak up for themselves."

ABU-L-QASIM AL-SHABBI (1909–1934) is considered Tunisia's most beloved poet of the twentieth century, despite his very short life. He was born in Tawzur in the palm grove district. His father was a judge and the family moved constantly from one town to another during al-Shabbi's childhood. At twelve, he was sent to study religion and linguistics in Tunis, where he later studied law. He started publishing when he was eighteen. Shortly after his marriage, he died of cardiac disease. His poetry is well known all over the Arab world.

HASHIM SHAFIQ was born and grew up in Iraq. He currently lives and writes poetry in Arabic in London.

ANTON SHAMMAS, the author of the novel *Arabesques*, is a Palestinian who writes in Arabic, Hebrew, and English. He lives in Ann Arbor, Michigan, with his wife, Rachel Persico, and their children, Alia and Nadeem.

SHAWQI ABI SHAQRA (b. 1935, Lebanon) worked as a teacher and journalist before becoming cultural editor for the leading Lebanese daily, *al-Nahar*. He is known for his experimentation, his prose poetry, and his support of young writers.

LAILA SHAWA (b. 1940, Palestine) has lived in Egypt, Rome, Austria, Beirut, and Gaza, where she worked with her father and husband to build the Rashad Shawa Cultural Center. Her paintings like "Impossible Dream" use decorative motifs, strong colors, and humor to convey a message about the social and political realities around her.

MOHAMMED SHEHADEH is a Palestinian poet and doctor living in Jerusalem.

REZA SHIRAZI is Iranian, grew up in India where he wrote his first poem about the Taj Mahal at the age of eight, and currently lives in Austin, Texas. He competes in triathlons.

MAHMUD M. SHURAYH (b. 1952, Lebanon) studied English and philosophy at the American University of Beirut. He has worked as a translator, teacher, writer on cultural affairs, and editor of modern Arabic poetry, and currently lives in France.

ARYEH SIVAN (b. 1929, Tel Aviv) lived near a beach of the Mediterranean until 1948. Later he studied at the Hebrew University in Jerusalem. He has published nine volumes of poetry and one novel and worked as a high school teacher until his retirement.

RONNY SOMECK (b. 1951, Baghdad) immigrated to Israel as a child. He has published seven collections of poems, including *Asphalt*, and many translations and received the Prime Minister's Prize in 1989.

NIDAL KAMAL TABAL (b. 1947, Syria) creates art that is inspired by the tradition of Arabic calligraphy, and uses the traditional Kufic script as a decorative art form. His work can be seen all over the Arab world, in public spaces, as wall decoration, and on buildings.

CHAIBIA TALLAL (b. 1929, Morocco) was married at thirteen and widowed two years later. She had no formal education or art training, and began her art career drawing on white bed sheets with the crayons her young son brought home from school. The director of the Modern Art Museum in Paris, Pierre Gaudibert, was impressed by her artwork and helped launch her career. Her work is exhibited throughout Europe and the Arab world.

ÜLKÜ TAMER (b. 1937, Turkey) works as a journalist and an actor, and translates poetry.

LINA TIBI is a Syrian poet.

GÖKHAN TOK (b. 1972, Ankara) graduated from the sociology department of the Middle East Technical University and is now working at The Turkish Foundation of Science and Research.

NADINE RACHID LAURE TOUMA writes: "There was, there was not a girl named Nadine. She was born in a small village in Lebanon called Kab-Elias, which means city of the sun. She had a limited childhood because the war in Lebanon started when she was two. One of her sweetest memories is sitting around the stove, *baboor*, in the middle of winter with snow falling outside, roasting potatoes and chestnuts. Eating *labneh* with bread, and listening to Teta's sister telling stories of lost kingdoms and love. Falling asleep on the sofa, and then being carried softly to bed while asking, 'Can I go play in the snow tomorrow, ya mama?'"

NADIA TUÉNI lived in Lebanon and died in 1983. She wrote many books of poems, including *Lebanon: Twenty Poems for One Love*, and was married to the former Ambassador of Lebanon to the United Nations.

KEMALETTIN TUĞCU (1902–1996) is one of the legends of Turkish popular writing. He was unable to walk and attended no schools. He wrote stories, poems, and novels, many about the grief of poor children, and eventually published more than 500 books. He considered himself "the richest man on earth" and wrote actively till his death, though he could barely hear or see in his last years.

FADWA TUQAN (b.1917, Palestine) grew up in the town of Nablus, where she still lives. Her brother Ibrahim, also a poet, gave her private lessons at home in lieu of formal secondary school. She learned English and took literature courses at Oxford, England. Her works became increasingly political as the Palestinian/Israeli conflict intensified. She has participated in poetry festivals all over the world and her works have been translated into numerous languages. She has received numerous honors and awards and is considered one of the treasures of the Arabic literary world.

REHA YALNIZCIK (b. 1950, Turkey) has worked as a freelance artist and an executive art director as well as a fine artist, and produced a children's television program. He lives in Istanbul with his wife and daughter.

SAADI YOUSSEF is one of the leading Iraqi poets, whose work is well known all over the Arab world. He currently resides in Paris.

BALKIS SALEEM ZAGHAL was born in Saudi Arabia and is a sixth grader now living in Tulkarm, the West Bank.

LORENE ZAROU-ZOUZOUNIS (b. 1958, Palestine) used to help her paternal grandmother sweep her patio, and pick wild herbs and greens in the fields near their home. She writes, "The smell of narcissus brings me home more than anything, as this flower filled the valleys and hills." She now lives in California with her American-Greek husband and their two daughters, Miriam and Athena.

FAHRELNISSA ZEID (1901–1991, Turkey) grew up in a family where books and art were valued. She studied in Istanbul and Paris, and had a distinguished career as a teacher and painter, founding the Fahrelnissa Zeid Royal Institute of Fine Arts in Jordan. Her works are exhibited in museums worldwide.

HELEN ZUGHAIB (Lebanon) has lived in Lebanon, Iraq, Kuwait, and the United States, and has exhibited her art widely. She hopes that her work can encourage dialogue and understanding between the cultures of the Arab world and the United States.

Distant stars
Are now in the palm of my hand
And we pluck them
And plant them in the carpet . . .
—Nava Semel

Intersection, Hassan al Mulla

Acknowledgments

I AM DEEPLY GRATEFUL to all who assisted this project so generously, passing addresses, poetry, and encouragement on to me, especially: Nathalie Handal, who seems to live everywhere at once, Sharif S. Elmusa, Khaled Mattawa, Assef al-Jundi, B.J. Fernea and Bruce Snider in Austin, and Yusuf Eradam and Asalet Erten in Turkey, Ambassador David M. Ransom in Bahrain, Bonnie Pales in Jordan, and Fereshteh Gol-Mohammadi in Iran. To all writers (especially Amina and Enshira al Bekri of Nablus), translators, and artists who sent work not included here, we apologize that this book could not be 1,000 pages long. There were many, many worthy choices.

The landmark labors of Dr. Salma Khadra Jayyusi of PROTA (Project of Translation from Arabic) have been an immense gift to our cultural heritage and we will never stop thanking her. Her anthologies are classics in the field.

My gratitude to: Barbara Nimri Aziz of Pacifica Radio in New York, Elie Chalala of *Al Jadid* magazine, the music of Hamza El Din and Simon Shaheen, poets Shirley Kaufman, Moshe Dor, Simon Lichman, and Karen Alkalay-Gut, to Samuel Hazo of the International Poetry Forum for everything, always, and to Kevin and Marilynn Rashid and David Watson who supplied fresh Arabic breads for ongoing sustenance from Dearborn. Also to Mustafa Hoş, Ammiel Alcalay, and Mira Meir for their help with the "calls for entries" mailings. Thanks to RAWI, the Radius of Arab American Writers, Inc, for spreading so many good words. Thanks to my father, Aziz Shihab, for his translations-on-demand, and my mother, Miriam Allwardt Shihab, for her proofreading eyes.

And very large hugs to the staff at Simon & Schuster Books for Young Readers: my luminous editor Virginia Duncan, her tireless associate editor Sarah Thomson, art director Lucille Chomowicz, and designer Anahid Hamparian. Their attention and care on this project could not have been dearer. Working with you is the best luck one could have in any life.

—*Naomi Shihab Nye*

The scope of this volume made it occasionally difficult—despite sincere and sustained effort—to locate a few of the poets and/or their executors. The compilers and editor regret any omissions or errors. If you wish to contact the publisher, corrections will be made in subsequent printings. Permission to reprint copyrighted material is gratefully acknowledged to the following:

MAMDOUH ADWAN, for excerpt from "Ziad's Little Moons," copyright © by Mamdouh Adwan. Printed by permission of the author.

MANSOUR AJAMI, for "Sumi's Infinity," copyright © by Mansour Ajami. Printed by permission of the author.

MANSOUR AJAMI, for "The Bridge" by Kaissar Afif, English translation copyright © by Mansour Ajami. Printed by permission of the translator. For "Quintrain" by Sa'id 'Aql.

AMMIEL ALCALAY, for "The Crusader Man" by Shelley Elkayam, English translation copyright © by Ammiel Alcalay, from *Keys To the Garden: New Israeli Writing*, published by City Lights, 1996. Printed by permission of the translator.

INDEX TO POETS AND ARTISTS

ÍNDEX TO POEMS

List of illustrations

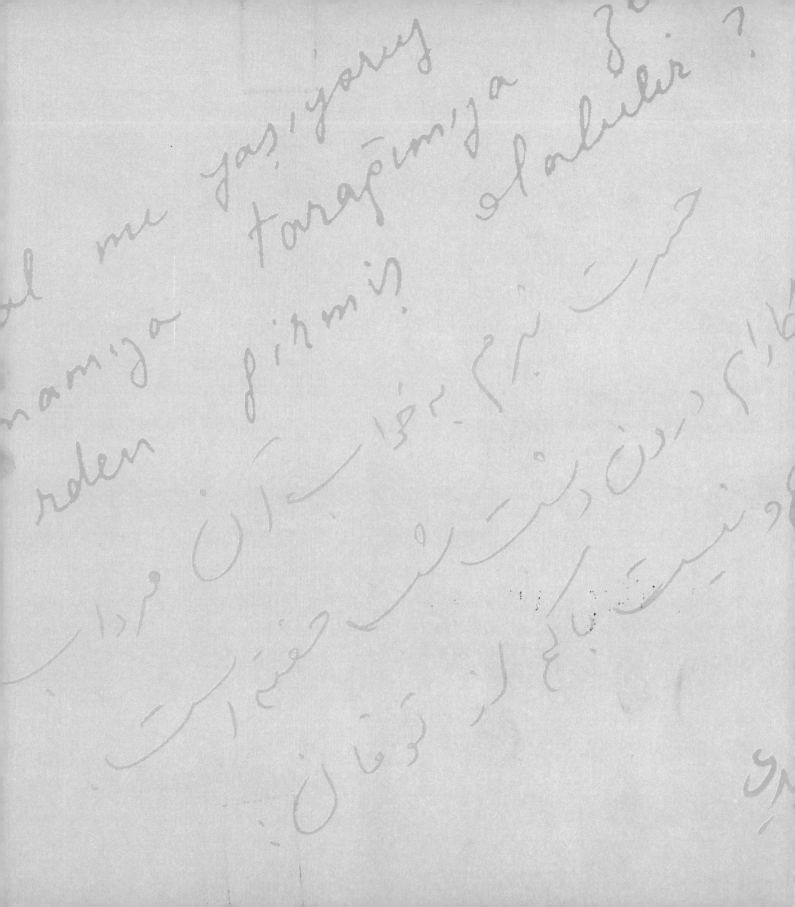

...l me yaşıyoruz
...namıza tarafımıza 38
...rden girmiş. olabilir?